# Thorkill of Iceland
# Viking Hero-Tales

# Thorkill of Iceland

## Viking Hero-Tales

Retold by Isabel Wyatt

Floris Books

Illustrated by Georgina McBain

*Thorkill of Icleand* first published in 1997.
*The Dream of King Alfdan* first published in 1961
by Follett Publishing Co, Chicago.
This edition published in 1997 by Floris Books, Edinburgh.
Reprinted 2001

British Library CIP Data available

ISBN 0-86315-256-2

Printed in Great Britain
by Biddles Ltd, Guildford

# Contents

## Thorkill of Iceland
*An Old Danish Hero-Tale*

## The Dream of King Alfdan
*An Old Norse Hero-Tale*

# Thorkill of Iceland

*An Old Danish Hero-Tale*

# How Thorkill came to King Gorm

When the Dusk of the Gods drew near its end, King Gorm the Old was King of Denmark.

He had sent his son, Prince Gotrik the Good, to the King of Frank-land to bring up. This was a thing kings did in the old days.

When Prince Gotrik was full-grown, he came back to King Gorm's hall. With him came Luf, his light-boy.

King Gorm had grown so old that he was like a child again. His will was so weak now that it swung to and fro like a weather-vane.

"Some lord is the wind that swings this weather-vane," Prince Gotrik said to Luf. "But which lord is it?"

It was Luf's task to bring the prince his wine-cup when he sat at meat, as well as to light him to bed. Luf had sharp eyes and ears. As he went to and fro in the hall, he kept eyes and ears wide open.

Luf had the gift of song-craft. From this he got his by-name of Luf the Lark. Each night, he held a lit torch when Prince Gotrik went to rest. As he did so, he put into a song the things he had seen that day.

One night, he sang this stave:

> Lord, do not trust
> A ring a-rust,
> A pot a-boil,
> A snake a-coil,
> A bear at play
> A bull at bay,
> A wolf in fold,

Ice one night old,
A root-less tree,
A waxing sea,
A bow that creaks,
A ship that leaks,
A half-burnt hall,
A head-strong thrall;
And, most of all,
Lord, do not trust the Fima-Feng!

"What do you mean by Fima-Feng?" asked Prince Gotrik.

For *Fima-Feng* means *Five-Fingers*. But it can also mean *Swift-to-Snatch*.

"That," said Luf the Lark, "is what I call the five lords who sit in a bunch on the bench, like the five fingers of a hand."

And he gave the five lords the names the boys in Frank-land gave to the five fingers:

Tall thin Long-Man,
Lick-Pot and Ring-Man,
Short thin Little-Man,
And short fat Thumb.

"And why must I not trust them?" asked Prince Gotrik.

"I think *they* are the wind that swings the weather-vane," said Luf. "I think they are the wind that blows the king's will this way and that to its own ends."

The next night, King Gorm sat at wine in his hall, with his hench-men and his bench-men.

As they drank and made merry, a blast was blown on the guest-horn that hung at the gate.

At a nod from the king, the man who was the door-guard that day drew back the bar that held the big door fast. Into the torch-lit hall, out of the night, came a stranger.

He was long and he was lean. He had keen blue eyes. He was clad in a bright helmet, a bright mail-coat, and a cloak of rich red fur.

It was clear he was no Dane. For his helmet had no boar on it.

It was clear that in his own land he must be a lord. For he held his head high, and his look was that of a man of noble birth.

Up the long hall he strode, to the old king on his high-seat.

"Hail, King Gorm!" he cried. "I am Thorkill of Iceland. May I be your guest this night?"

All down the long wall-bench, from man to man, flew the name:

"Thorkill of Iceland! It is the hero, Thorkill of Iceland!"

For Thorkill was a name famous over all the North-Lands.

Up sprang Prince Gotrik from his place at King Gorm's side. He was glad indeed to give up his seat to so brave a hero as Thorkill.

Up sprang Luf from his stool at Prince Gotrik's feet. He was glad indeed to bear the guest-cup to so brave a hero as Thorkill.

"I am glad to see you in my hall, Thorkill," said King Gorm. "You have visited many lands, and seen many marvels. Sit, now, and tell me of them."

For King Gorm's joy in new marvels was one of the few joys left to him, now that he had grown so old.

So Thorkill sat down by King Gorm, and told him of marvel after marvel he had seen.

11

The old king's face lit up as he drank in the stories, and his dim old eyes grew bright. And Luf, at Thorkill's feet, drank them in with as much joy as the king.

"Stay with me, Thorkill," cried King Gorm, "not as a night-guest, but for as long as you may. It is long since guest came to my hall with so many new marvels to tell of!"

Then Luf's quick eyes saw how snake-keen grew the eyes of the Fima-Feng. He saw how the five heads of the five lords drew into a tight bunch, and began to wag one at the other.

"If Thorkill stays," said Long-Man, "our grip on the king will be lost. He must be got rid of. But how?"

"*We* must get rid of him," said Lick-Pot. "But how?"

"We must bend the king to send him away," said Ring-Man. "But how?"

"We must get Thorkill to tell of such marvels," said Little-Man, "that the king will not rest till he has sent him to seek them out."

"But let them be such as only Thorkill can seek," said Thumb, "lest we find *we* are sent."

Then Luf saw how the five lords began to spin a net to catch the king's will.

"Is it true, Thorkill," asked Long-Man, "that your birth-land lies on the outer rim of Middle-Earth?"

"It is," said Thorkill. "If a man sails north past Iceland, he sails into the Sea that Rings the Earth. Not till sun and stars are left behind will he reach land again, and only then with luck."

"What land will he reach?" asked Lick-Pot.

And Thorkill told him: "The first of the five vast tracts of Giant-land."

The news flew from lip to lip all down the long hall: "Giant-land! Thorkill tells of Giant-land!"

"Is it true, as men say," asked Ring-Man, "that in Giant-land are marvels such as few men have ever seen?"

"In Iceland men tell of such marvels," said Thorkill. "But I have yet to meet a man who has seen them."

The old king's eyes grew bright. "What marvels?" he asked. "Tell me of some of them, Thorkill!"

And Thorkill told him: "One such marvel is Garfred's Treasure-Town. Men say that in this town stands Garfred's Treasure-Hall, as big as seven hills and full to the roof of treasure such as men see only in dreams. And amid his hills of treasure sits Garfred the Giant, in a deep sleep."

Then cried Little-Man to King Gorm: "Lord, why not send Thorkill to fetch you some of this treasure, that you may see this marvel with your own eyes?"

At this the old king's eyes grew still more bright.

But Thorkill said: "Men may not take away this treasure. A dread doom falls on any man who lays a finger on it. Men may only go and gaze."

"Then, Lord," said Thumb, "let Thorkill go and gaze, and bring you back news of this marvel."

Then Luf the Lark bore a wine-cup to Prince Gotrik. He bent over it to hiss to him:

"Lord, Five-Fingers are Swift-to-Snatch!
A net is set, the king to catch!"

Then Prince Gotrik saw the way things went. And to try to save Thorkill, he asked: "But is it also true, Thorkill, as men say, that a man in Giant-land bears his life in his hand?"

And Thorkill told him: "True it is, Prince Gotrik. A

far-off land is Giant-land, a dark land, a land of witch-craft. So full is it of traps and pit-falls that a man needs to be brave and bold and good and lucky if he is ever to come back!"

At this, the light died out of the old king's eyes. He said with a sigh: "Then, for all my joy in such marvels, I will not send you to seek them, Thorkill. I will not risk the life of so dear a hero in such a quest."

So, for that time, Luf the Lark and Prince Gotrik the Good were able to save Thorkill.

# How King Gorm sent Thorkill to Giant-land

But the Fima-Feng did not give up. When the king went to rest, the five lords left the hall. Down to the sea-strand the five lords went. They sat on the rocks in the moon-light, as near to each other as the fingers of a hand.

And they began to plot how they might yet get rid of Thorkill.

"What we must find," said Long-Man, "is a thing so dear to the king that he will risk even Thorkill's life for it."

"I can think of one such thing," said Lick-Pot. "So old is King Gorm, he is near to the end of his days. Yet he fears to die, for he knows of no abode of the gods the dead can go to now. To get news of such an abode, he will risk even a hero's life."

"Then let us put it into his mind," said Ring-Man, "to send Thorkill to get this news."

"Let us put it into his mind," said Little-Man, "to send Thorkill to ask of King Gorm's own god, Utgard-Loki. For even for Thorkill, to find a god will be a task to fill the rest of his life-time."

"And *if* he finds him," said Thumb, "he finds his own doom. For Thorkill, by his name, is hench-man to Thor. And never were two such foes as Thor and Utgard-Loki. So will not Utgard-Loki slay Thorkill, if ever they come face to face?"

"He will!" cried the rest of the Fima-Feng. "And we shall be well rid of him."

The next night, as they all sat at wine with the king, Luf saw how the five lords began to spin a new net to catch the king's will.

Said Long-Man: "The Dusk of the Gods took the gods of Asgard from us, and it took Asgard with them. I wonder what abode of the gods a man can go to now when he dies?"

Said Lick-Pot: "In the old days, men of war such as we are went to Odin in Asgard. But at the Dusk, Odin was slain, and Asgard was burnt. And there is no other abode of the gods known to men here in Denmark. Is any known to men in Iceland, Thorkill?"

Then said Thorkill: "We know of one from old songs our glee-men sing, songs that tell of the Dusk and of a new God who is to end it. This new God will make a new Asgard, all of gems. Gem-Lea, the old songs call it. And all men will be free to go to Gem-Lea when life on Earth is over."

Then said Ring-Man: "But the new God has not come as yet, and the new Asgard is not built. Then to what abode of the gods can *we* go when we die?"

Then said Prince Gotrik: "The new God may have come and have made the new Asgard by the time our death-hour finds us."

"You are still standing at the door of life, Prince," said Little-Man. "So for you this well may be. But not for us who are so near its end."

Then said King Gorm with a sigh: "And least of all for a man as old as I. But *can* any man know this thing? It seems to me a riddle too deep for the wit of man."

"It *is* too deep for the wit of man," said Thumb. "Only the gods can know it. Yet no god is left to know it."

"Except for my god, Utgard-Loki," said the king.

Then asked Thorkill: "Is Utgard-Loki a god, then, here in Denmark? In Iceland we call him only king of the old giants."

"He is all that is left from the days of the old gods," said Long-Man. "So he is the only god men have — till your new God is come."

"Can we not send and ask *him* this riddle?" asked Lick-Pot. "For we who love the king can see it is one that will not let him rest."

"I would send swiftly enough," said King Gorm, "if I could find a man who knows the way."

Then Ring-man turned to Thorkill.

"You call Utgard-Loki a giant, Thorkill, " he said. "Then does he not dwell in Giant-land?"

And Thorkill answered: "In Iceland men say that he dwells in the Land of Utgard, the fifth vast country at the far north tip of Giant-land. But never yet did I hear of a man had been so far."

"Never yet did I even hear of a man who knew as much as this!" cried Little-man. "Today our king meets a new marvel — a man who knows the way to Utgard-Loki!"

"Here at your side, Lord," cried Thumb, "sits the one man in all the land fit to send on this high mission! It seems he must have come to Denmark just to set your mind at rest!"

Then Luf the Lark bore a wine-cup to Prince Gotrik. He bent over it to hiss to him:

> "Lord, strike to foil
> Five snakes a-coil!"

Then Prince Gotrik saw the way things went. And to try to save Thorkill, he asked: "What of the traps and pit-falls? Did you not say, my father, that you must not risk the life of so dear a hero on such a mission?"

"But that time we spoke of the search for treasure, Gotrik," said the weak old king. "We speak now of a search for gods."

"Yet the same traps and pit-falls strew the way," said Prince Gotrik. "What good to send a man for news he is not able to bring back?"

"Did not Thorkill say," said Long-Man, "that a man must be brave and bold and good and lucky if he was ever to come back? Then Thorkill *will* come back! For is he not all this?"

At this, the old king's face lit up.

"That is well said!" he cried. "If ever any man was brave and bold and good and lucky, Thorkill is that man. So I will send you to Utgard-Loki, Thorkill, to bring me back this news."

"And will it not be well, Lord," said Lick-Pot, "for Thorkill to look at the treasure on the way, and bring you *that* news, also?"

"It will," said the king. "I send you, Thorkill, on a twofold search!"

Then said Ring-Man: "We wish you swift winds, Thorkill! May you come soon to Utgard-Loki!"

And each of the five lords put his hand to his lips, to hide a sin-sly grin.

In this way did the Fima-Feng bend the old king's will to its own ends.

In this way, in spite of Luf the Lark and Prince Gotrik the Good, the five lords found a way to get Thorkill sent from Denmark.

# How Thorkill got his ship

Then said Thorkill to King Gorm: "Lord, if ever a man had need of a stout ship, I shall have need of such a ship on this quest. For it must stand up to wind and storm such as you have never seen in your kind home-seas."

"You shall have it," said King Gorm. "Ask what you will for your ship, and it shall be yours."

"First," said Thorkill, "I shall need stout oak planks for the frame."

"Then let us go to my oak-woods," said King Gorm, "and you shall pick out the trees to fell for the planks. It will give me such joy to see this quest-ship grow."

Then said Luf the Lark to Prince Gotrik: "Lord, let us go too."

So to the king's oak-woods they all four went.

"This is a stout oak, Lord Thorkill! And this, and this!" cried Luf.

"Yes, so I think, too," said Thorkill. And he put his mark on the trees.

"Next," said Thorkill, "I shall need a tall fir for the mast."

"Then let us go to my fir-woods," said King Gorm, "and you shall pick out the tree for the mast."

Then said Luf the Lark to Prince Gotrik: "Lord, let us go, too."

So to the king's fir-woods they all four went.

"This is the best fir in the wood, Lord Thorkill!" cried Luf.

"Yes, so I think, too," said Thorkill. And he put his mark on the tree.

"Now," said Thorkill, "I shall need sails."

"Then let us look at my cloak-chests," said King Gorm, "and you shall pick out your sails."

For in the old days the North-men set cloaks on the masts for sails. That was why, when they came to make real sails later, they still wove them with a stripe, like cloaks.

Then said Luf the Lark to Prince Gotrik: "Lord, let us look, too."

So to the king's cloak-chests they all four went.

Luf ran and threw back the lids of the chests for the king.

"Those with the blue and white stripes, Lord Thorkill," said Luf, "will look well against a blue and white sky."

"Yes, so I think, too," said Thorkill. And those were the cloaks he chose.

Then they all four went to the king's hemp-fields. And Luf chose the hemp to make the ropes for the ship.

Then they all four went to the king's tan-yards. And Luf chose the hides to roof the deck of the ship.

Then they all four went to the king's smithy. And Luf blew the fire for the smith, as he made bolts and bars and nails for the ship.

In this way, Luf chose all the things Thorkill had need of for the ship.

It gave the old king such joy to see the ship grow; but not more joy than it gave to Luf the Lark.

They saw the trees cut down with ringing axes. They saw them sawed into stout planks with rasping saws. They saw the frame of the ship take form under clanging hammers.

They saw the king's shipwrights stuff the seams of the frame with cord of spun goat-hair. They saw them stamp the goat-hair deep into the seams, to make them water-tight.

With gay stamp and tramp, Luf stamped the goat-hair in with them.

They went to see the king's wood-carver shape and carve the prow of the ship. Luf took up a tool to help him, with much joy in this new craft.

The wood-carver asked Thorkill: "Lord, what head will you have for the prow? A dragon? A griffin? A fish? A snake? A bird?"

"Let the ship be a swan, Lord Thorkill!" cried Luf. "A red and gold swan, with white and blue sails for wings!"

"Let it be a swan," said Thorkill.

So Luf and the wood-carver made the prow rise up in a tall swan's neck, with a swan's head to crown it.

Then Luf asked Thorkill: "What name will you give your ship, Lord?"

"This ship seems to be rather yours than mine," said Thorkill. "So you shall name her for me."

"Then I shall call her *Sun-Swan*, Lord," said Luf.

"A good name," said Thorkill. "*Sun-Swan* she shall be."

Then Thorkill took up a tool, to cut a rune of good luck along the beak of the swan-prow.

Luf stood by, and spelt out the rune as he cut it.

"What! Can you read runes, boy?" asked Thorkill.

"See if I can, Lord," said Luf. And he read out the rune Thorkill had cut:

> May flood be no foe to you!
> May good luck flow to you!

May fair winds blow to you!
May all things ill to you
Turn to good-will to you!"

And so at last, out of oak and fir, and hide and hemp, and tar and pitch, and iron and bronze, and silk and wool and goat-hair, and red clay-stain and pure gold-leaf, came *Sun-Swan,* full-grown.

Long and strong, yet light and slight and full of grace, she lay at rest on smooth rollers at the edge of King Gorm's haven, just out of reach of the sea.

Never had King Gorm seen such a ship. Never had Luf the Lark. Never had any Dane of all the vast throng that came to the sea-shore to see her.

For *Sun-Swan* was a hundred feet from stem to stern. Amidships, she was thirty feet from side to side. She had forty strakes of stout oak planks each side, held fast with tree-nails and black-metal bolts.

Her fir-tree mast was forty feet high. It was set in a deep oak block in the midst of the ship. It sprang to and fro, as a tree rocks; yet it stood as firm as if strong roots went down into the deck.

*Sun-Swan* had space for thirty oars each side. Each oar was twenty feet long, with oars longer yet at the prow and the stern, that rose high out of the water.

*Sun-Swan* had a deck-roof of ox-hides, to keep out the spray. She had a fire-pit to cook food. She had pots to cook food in; she had spits to cook food on. She had dippers, to bale with. She had a hold full of arms for the shipmen. She had nets and fish-spears; she had chess-men and dice.

In her food-holds, *Sun-Swan* had many a fat flitch of smoke-dried ham. She had many a pole hung with wind-dried strips of fish. She had many a sack of grain and keg of butter to make brose; and many a chest of meal to make bread; and many a vast pot of whale-oil.

At the top of her tall mast, her gilt wind-vane swung with glint of gold. All gold and red rose the long swan-neck of her prow. And from the high swan-head to the high curl of the stern, both sides of her were hung with shields. One black, one gold, one black, one gold, they hung in two long rows.

"I have got my ship," said Thorkill. "And now I must get my shipmen."

# How Thorkill got his shipmen

When Thorkill said that now he must get his shipmen,
Luf stood on one leg, and cast a look up at Prince Gotrik.

Prince Gotrik said: "This sprig of a lad is wild to go
with you, Thorkill. Will you take him off my hands?"

"Oho!" said Thorkill. "And what do you know of ship-
craft, Luf the Lark?"

Then Luf stood up on his two feet, and put back his
head, and sang:

> "When I was small,
> I stood at my father's knee,
> And sang him songs
> Like one grown old in skald-craft.
> Men gave me then
> My by-name, the Lark;
> And for name-gift,
> My father gave me a boat
> With ten fair oars,
> And ten thralls' sons,
> As old as I was, to ply them.
> Then high at the helm stood I
> To steer my bark,
> And so wend home to his haven.
>
> *What do you know of ship-craft?*
> Asks my lord.
> I can steer, and row, and bale,
> And furl a sail.
> I can join the fray

In the strands of a rope
With sea-knots.
Neat needle-man am I
When the wind's teeth slit a sail.
I can climb the mast,
A-swing in the storm,
And look for land from the gilt-vane.
I can skip to and fro
On the oars as they row,
To make the oarsmen merry.
I can sing a stave
In wave on wave,
For the oarsmen to keep time to — "

Thorkill put up his hand to stop the flow.

"How can I *not* take such a lark?" he cried. "Did I not say it was rather your ship than mine? Let us go now, and seek the oarsmen you are to sing to."

So down went Luf and Thorkill to the vast throng of men at the lip of the sea.

"I seek shipmen," Thorkill told them. "Who wants to sail to Giant-land with me?"

"Lord, I!" — "And I, Lord!" — "And I!" went up the cry.

"You know of the storms we must face?" asked Thorkill.

"In so stout a ship we shall make light of storms," cried back the men.

"You know of the traps and pit-falls the giants set for men?" asked Thorkill.

"We can face them, led by a hero," cried the men.

"You know we may never come back?" asked Thorkill.

"Small is the risk, with one who is brave and bold and good and lucky," cried the men.

So from the throng Thorkill chose as many shipmen as he and *Sun-Swan* had need of. He drew them up in rows on the sea-strand. One by one, and rank by rank, he spoke with them, to find out from each man what craft he had been bred to.

He chose sixty men to man the oars. He chose two twin-brothers, Gok and Bok, to be ship's cook and store-master. He chose two other twin-brothers, Onni and Omd, to take turns with him at the helm. He chose Aldi to be fire-keeper. He chose Sild to be arms-smith.

To each of his shipmen Thorkill gave a bear-skin cloak.

"Keep it with care," he told them. "You will need it when we reach Frost-giant-land."

To each of his shipmen Thorkill gave a flint and a spike of steel.

"Keep them with care," he told them. "If *Sun-Swan* sinks, and you are cast up on a shore far from men, you will need them, to make fire."

And now Thorkill had his ship and his shipmen.

"Let us set out on our quest," he said.

All the king's lords and all the king's men came in a huge throng to the harbour, to see *Sun-Swan* put out to sea.

King Gorm set a rare gold cup in Thorkill's hands.

"When you ask Utgard-Loki my riddle," he said, "give this to him from me."

Prince Gotrik drew an arm-ring from his own arm, and set it on Thorkill's. The arm-ring was of thick gold. A rich red gem was set in it.

"The gem glows in the dark," he said. "It may be of help to you when sun and stars are left behind."

Then Thorkill held his arm high, and hench-men and bench-men sprang to the side of *Sun-Swan*. A strong push; a long push; then a cheer went up as the ship slid off the smooth rollers and into the sea.

It was a bright day; the swan-prow was as gay with gold as the sun in a clear sky. Thorkill stood at the helm, with Luf the Lark at his side. The shipmen let out the blue and white sails to catch the wind. The oarsmen sat at the oars.

"Start *Sun-Swan's* first oar-song, Luf," said Thorkill. We will each sing a verse in turn."

Then Luf began his oar-song. With a splash of sixty oars, with a play of shield on shield, the red prow clove the blue wave, as *Sun-Swan* put out to sea.

Under the black and gold shields, the long oars rose and fell, rose and fell, to the beat of the verse Luf sang:

> "*Sun-Swan* puts out to sea.
> Her swan's down is ground gold.
> Gold glints the gilt
> Of the wind-vane at her mast-head.
> She lets the gold from her swan-prow
> Shine down upon the wave.
> *Sun-Swan* puts out to sea."

Thorkill sang the next verse. Under the black and gold shields, the long oars rose and fell, rose and fell, to the beat of the verse he sang:

> "*Sun-Swan* puts out to sea.
> Out leap her sails,
> Snow-white, with bands of blue.
> Her red prow speeds over the whale-path.
> With a snap of oar-thongs,
> Her oarsmen bend to the oars.
> Under the swell of the sails,

They shave the foam with brisk oar-blades.
With one smooth oar-stroke,
Sixty oars smite the sea.
*Sun-Swan* puts out to sea."

Luf sang the next verse. Under the black and gold
shields, the long oars rose and fell, rose and fell, to the
beat of the verse he sang:

"*Sun-Swan* puts out to sea.
Over the splash of oars,
Over the ring of shield-clang,
High swells my song-wave.
For we have high deeds to do.
Beyond the skirts of the Earth
Must *Sun-Swan* swim.
The lore she will bear back
Shall live in the minds of men
As long as men live.
The tale of Sun-Swan
Shall last as long as men dwell
In the lands of the North.
*Sun-Swan* puts out to sea."

So out to sea swam Sun-Swan; and in the harbour,
King Gorm and his men stood to see her go. A little
apart from the rest, as near to each other as the fingers
of a hand, stood the five lords of the Fima-Feng.

They stood till *Sun-Swan* had shrunk to a toy ship
on the skyline. Then each gave the others a wink and
a sin-sly grin.

"May that be the last we shall see of our Thorkill!"
said Long-Man.

"It will be!" said Thumb.

# How Thorkill got to Giant-land

North swam *Sun-Swan*. Soon Thorkill, at the helm, saw land rise to the East.

"Lord, what land is that?" asked Luf.

And Thorkill told him: "Norway."

North still swam *Sun-Swan,* up the long zig-zag stretch of rocks and cliffs and crags that was the coast of Norway.

Each night, the shipmen saw the Pole Star over them. Each day, they drew in to land, and got fresh spring-water, and made a fire on the shore, for Gok the Cook to bake bread and roast fresh meat.

"Let us eat fresh meat while we may," said Thorkill. "While we may let us drink fresh spring-water. The time will come when we shall be far from land. Then our meat must be dried meat, and our water rain-water."

North still swam *Sun-Swan,* past the north-most tip of Norway. North still swam *Sun-Swan,* till Thorkill, at the helm, saw a black mass far off on the sky-line to the West.

"Lord, what land is that?" asked Luf.

And Thorkill told him: "Iceland."

"Will you stop at your birth-right land on the way, Lord?" asked Luf.

"If it *were* on the way, but it is not," said Thorkill.

And still North swam *Sun-Swan,* and still North, and still North, till she came into a sea with a wall of waves. They stood on end all round it like steep cliffs, as still as stone.

"Lord, what sea is this?" asked Luf.

And Thorkill told him: "The Sea that Rings the Earth."

And still North swan *Sun-Swan,* to the tall sea-walls. By night, white waves of light ran over the dark sky. By this floodlight, the shipmen saw the steep cliffs of water grow near, more near, and at last loom right over them.

"Row, now, for dear life!" cried Thorkill.

The men plied the oars with power. The sails blew out. With blue and white wings spread, *Sun-Swan* sprang at the sea-walls.

The roar was loud as the sea-walls fell on the ship. *Sun-Swan* was thrust into a deep pit of foam. With a clang of shields, she was flung out from the pit. Then she slid into a soft swell of water, as smooth as a pool.

By the white throbs of light, the shipmen saw the sea gush up, to pile again into steep cliffs, as still as stone. But now *Sun-Swan* swam out of reach, on the far side of them.

"What harm did the sea-walls do to us?" Thorkill asked Luf.

With his flint and steel, Luf lit a torch of dried rush, and ran to find out.

The sails were rent. The deck was under water. A flood in the fire-pit had put out the fire.

"Small harms are they," said Thorkill. "We have had good luck so far. Bid Aldi light a new fire. Bid the bale-men bale out the water. On the rent sails, when it is day, you shall show us your skill as needle-man."

Still North swam Sun-Swan, under the swell of the sails and the drive of smooth, swift oar-strokes. Still bright with gold was she; her red prow cast red gleams in the still water; and in her wake were the white tracks of her oars.

But now a wind sprang up. It grew fresh. The fresh wind grew to a gale. The gale grew to a storm.

It drove the sails out from the stays; it tore them to shreds. With a snap of sail-yards, the forty-foot stem of the mast began to thresh to and fro.

The shipmen ran to the ropes, to furl the sails. The bale-men ran to bale.

Suck and surge, wave fell on wave, in heap on heap. The sea gaped open to swallow the ship. It drove her this way and that.

The tree-nails sprang under the strain. The spars bent. The ribs of the ship began to groan. The stout oak planks were rent apart as if they were but birch-bark. The tide swept the deck. It tore the men from the oars.

Thorkill, still at the helm, sent Luf to Bok the Store-Master.

"Bid Bok get me six pots of whale-oil from the store," he told him. Back ran Luf, with his men to bear the six large pots of whale-oil.

The wild tide beat Gok down. It split the doors of the foodhold as he tried to bar them. Into the holds burst the sea.

Meat and meal, grain and butter and poles of fish were swept in a stream over the side of the ship. They were lost in the pitch and toss of the waves. They sank in the deep black water.

Then over the rim of the helm-rail, Thorkill broke the six large pots of whale-oil, pot by pot. The oil spread in a film on the sea; and as far as it spread, the sea grew still.

And he kept *Sun-Swan* in that still patch, while all round it the wild black sea shot up to meet the wild grey sky, then fell with a crash into deep wells, churning wild white foam.

In time, the storm wore its own rage out. The wind fell. The waves fell.

Thorkill, still at the helm, asked Luf: "What cheer, my lad?"

Luf, pale and spent, drew in a deep breath.

"Hale hands, Lord," he said, "but no sea-legs!"

From the shipmen, storm-worn, storm-torn, went up a loud shout of mirth. Each wept with the smart of brine on his eyelids; but each face, stiff with salt, split in a grin of glee. They went to and fro, to mend ropes and spars and sails, to clear the deck, to bar the holds, to put *Sun-Swan* ship-shape. But each time two met, one sang out to the other: "What cheer, my lad?"

And the other sang back: "Hale hands, Lord, but no sea-legs!"

Bok the Store-Master came to Thorkill, to count up in food the cost of that storm.

"Lord, most of our store of meat is lost," he told him, "and much butter, and much grain."

"Eke out the foods we are short of, as much as you can," Thorkill said. "And give out nets and fish-spears, and let the men fish."

Still North swam *Sun-Swan*. Each day, Thorkill made a cut on the helm-rail with a slash of his sword, to mark the days. Each day, the shipmen had less meat to eat. Each day, the light grew more and more dim, till even at high noon the air was grey.

Then Bok the Store-Master came again to Thorkill.

"Lord, we have no more meat," he told him. "Our store of meal is all that is left."

"Then let Gok feed us on bread and fish, Bok," said Thorkill. "It will not be for long. The day-light grows so dark that we shall soon have left sun and stars behind. And when we do, we shall sight land."

All that the men spoke of now, as they bent to the oars, was the lack of meat, and the feast of it they saw ahead, when they came again to land.

"Goat-flesh is what I long for," said one.

"And I for a fine fat sheep," said the next.

"A fine fat buck for me," said the next.

"Or a fine fat wood-bear," said the next.

And the next asked Thorkill: "What fine fat beasts do you think we shall find, Lord, when we come to land?"

"At the least," said Thorkill, "we shall pick puffin bones."

As the roar of mirth died down, Luf cried: "Hark, Lord! Do you not hear a new sound?"

Thorkill laid his brow to *Sun-Swan's* neck, his eyes shut, his ears a-strain. Then, with a slow nod of his head, he told them: "It is true. It is the beat of surf on a shore!"

A shout of joy went up from the men; and Luf began to skip on the bows of the oars, and to lilt:

> "It is the beat of surf on a strand!
> Men, your puffins are at hand!
> Up with you, Luf, to the gilt-vane,
> And tell us when you sight land!"

And he sprang from the oars to the mast; and up he went, hand over hand.

"Land ahoy!" he cried, as he clung, aloft, to the gilt-vane.

Again a shout went up from the men; and with such a will did they bend to the oars that *Sun-Swan* began to bound over the foam.

Down the mast to the deck slid Luf.

"So, Lord!" he cried. "We have got to Giant-land!"

# How Thorkill came
# to Herd-giant-land

"Rest on your oars, men," said Thorkill. "The tide will drift us in."

Glad were the shipmen to rest on the oars, and in the dim light to turn keen eyes to scan the sky-line for the first sight of land.

When it came, a shout of joy went up again.

The shipmen were still glad to rest on the oars, and to stare and to stare and to stare at that black streak on the sky-line.

In the dim light, they saw the black streak grow into a dark grey mass.

Is the dim light, they saw the dark grey mass turn to a strip of brown sand, with a strip of green grass beyond it, and, beyond the strip of green grass, a tall wall of black cliffs.

Now a loud shout of joy went up from the men. For now, all over the strip of green grass, they saw red and white specks that soon grew into toy cattle.

"A strand-hew!" A strand-hew!" they cried.

Thorkill spoke then in a grave tone:

"Men, you shall hold a strand-hew, for it is long since you had fresh meat. But bear in mind the law of strand-hew. Shipmen may hew down cattle upon any strand they come to. But cattle for one meal only."

"Yes, yes, Lord," cried the men, but with a shrug, and with eyes still on the cattle.

"If we slay more," Thorkill went on, "the herd-master can ask what fine he will, and we must pay it."

"If he asks too much, we can slay *him!*" cried one of the men.

"Think you so?" said Thorkill in a dry tone. "Bear in mind that this herd-master will be a giant!"

But the shipmen gave scant heed. A cheer went up as they felt *Sun-Swan* grate on the strand. Over her sides they slid, and down the ropes that hung swaying below the rows of shields.

Up on the beach they drew *Sun-Swan*. Then on to dry land they ran. Over the brown sand they ran. Up, up, they ran, to the red and white cattle grazing on the green grass.

The cattle were fat and well-fed. They were tame, and full of trust. They stood still to look with wild eyes at the shipmen. They stood still as the men fell on them, dagger in hand.

One by one, the cattle were hewn down. In spite of Thorkill's shouts, the shipmen went on with the strand-hew till all the herd were slain.

Then to and fro on the strand ran the shipmen, to pick up drift-wood. With flint and steel, fire after fire was lit. At each fire they set meat to roast, on daggers and swords for spits.

At each fire they left a ship-man to see the meat cook. Back and forth to the ship ran the others, to fill the food-holds with what was left of the strand-hew.

Then round each fire in a ring they sat, and took the meat each cook gave them. As they ate, they sang and made merry. Then down on the strand they lay, to sleep off the feast.

But a roar from the cliff-top made each ship-man sit up with a jerk, made each head turn to look. Down a steep path from the cliff-top, they saw a long file of giants rush, each with a club in his hand. So vast were they, it was as if a row of towers swept down on them.

Up sprang the shipmen, with cries of fear.

"We must flee!" cried some.

And down the strand to *Sun-Swan* they ran.

"We must fight!" cried some.

And they bent to snatch up the swords and daggers that lay about the fires. But Thorkill stood still with Luf at his side, and with Gok and Bok, Onni and Omd, and Aldi and Sild about him.

"We will not flee and we will not fight," said Thorkill. "We broke the law of strand-hew. We will pay the fine."

With a splash, *Sun-Swan* slid back into the foam. The men who had fled bent to the oars; and the ship ran out to sea.

But Thorkill stood still, his back to the sea, his eyes on the giants.

At the first of the fires the giants came to a halt. Thorkill and Luf and the men who stood with them saw the giants step round the fire, then poke at the fire, then hold out vast hands to its heat.

Then on along the strand they came.

"Let each man lift his hands, held flat, like mine," said Thorkill, "to show we hide no arms."

This they all did.

As the giants drew near, the first one set his vast hand to his vast brow to look out to sea.

"Are you master of that ship?" he asked Thorkill.

"I am," said Thorkill.

"Did you bid the men in it take it?" asked the giant.

"I did not," said Thorkill.

"Have you still need of it?" asked the giant.

"I have," said Thorkill.

"Then you shall have it," said the giant.

And out into the sea, in the wake of *Sun-Swan,* he began to wade.

Never did the oarsmen row as they did now. Each man bent full on his back. So hard did they row that the oar-thongs split.

But with stride on slow stride, the giant came up to the ship. The sea came only to his hip, and his head rose as high as the gilt-vane at her mast-head.

The men in the ship cast a flight of spears. But the giant felt no more than thorn-pricks. He set his vast hand on *Sun-Swan's* prow; the slight push he gave her sent her back to land.

Then back to land came the giant, stride by slow stride.

"Will you have the shipmen on the strand?" he asked Thorkill.

"I will," said Thorkill.

Then each of the giants bent over *Sun-Swan.* Each took up a man from the oar-bench in each vast hand, and set him down on the strand, till all his shipmen stood with Thorkill.

"Now, Ship-Master!" said the giant. "Your men have slain all our herd."

"They have," said Thorkill.

"The law of strand-hew has not been kept," said the giant.

"It has not," said Thorkill.

"Will you pay the fine we set?" asked the giant.

"We will," said Thorkill.

The giant put up his vast hand to scratch his vast head.

"What is this hot red thing your men left on the strand?" he asked.

"That is fire," said Thorkill.

"How is it born?" asked the giant.

"I will show you," said Thorkill.

And to Luf he said: "Bring me drift-wood." Luf ran and did so.

Then Thorkill took out his flint and his steel; and struck a spark with them. The spark fell on the drift-wood; and Thorkill bent and blew. The spark grew to a small flame. The small flame grew to a big flame. The big flame fed on the drift-wood.

The fire was lit.

At this, all the giants began to rub vast hands with glee.

"Fire is a fine thing to have," said the first giant.

"It is," said Thorkill.

"The strand-hew fine," said the giant, "shall be one such fire-stone and one such fire-stick for each man."

"That is too much," said Thorkill. "That is all we have. And we, too, need them when we wish to make fire. Take all save ten."

"Then you must give us ten of your men as well," said the giant.

"Take all save three," said Thorkill.

"Then you must give us three of your men," said the giant.

"Take all save one," said Thorkill.

"Then you must give us one of your men," said the giant.

"Hold out your hand," said Thorkill, with a sigh.

The giant held out his vast hand.

Then to his men Thorkill said: "Go past the giant one by one. As you pass him, each must drop his flint and steel into the giant's hand."

This the men did. At the end came Thorkill, and put his own flint and steel on top of all the rest.

Then the other giants each took up a shipman in each vast hand, and set him back on the ship. When all were on deck, they gave *Sun-Swan* a push. With a clash of shield on shield, out she shot into the foam.

Then the oarsmen were glad to make the blades slash in and out of the sea. Swift was the speed of Sun-Swan as she drew away from Herd-giant-land.

Then Thorkill sent Luf to bring Aldi the Fire-Keeper to him.

When Aldi came, Thorkill told him: "From now on, you must keep in the ship-fire night and day. Never must it go out. For now we have not one flint and steel to make a fresh fire with."

"Dear did we pay for our puffin bones, Lord!" said Luf.

# How Thorkill came to Fire-giant-land

Still North swam Sun-Swan. By day she swam now in a grey fog, by night in a black pit.

The shipmen now saw no sun by day. By night they saw no stars. They had left sun and stars behind them.

Even by day, each man now saw the next man as just a grey form in the grey gloom. Only Thorkill stood out from the rest. For now the red gem in Prince Gotrik's arm-ring began to glow like a small red fire.

Now Aldi the Fire-Keeper kept the ship-fire in the fire-pit going, night and day.

But one grey day, he came to Thorkill.

"Lord,", he said, "to keep the fire burning night and day consumes our fuel store far too swiftly. It we do not soon come to land and get in fresh store of it, we shall have no fuel left."

"Then let the fire sink as low as you can, so long as it keeps burning," said Thorkill. "Let it be big only when Gok needs it so, to cook the strand-hew meat."

This Aldi did. But in a few days he came again to Thorkill.

"Lord," he said, "the strand-hew meat is at an end. But so is the fire, if I can find no more wood. And Gok has still need of a good fire, to bake bread."

"Then you must burn such wood from the frame of the ship, said Thorkill, "as it is safe to take."

This Aldi did. With this wood for some days he fed the fire. Then again he came to Thorkill.

"Lord," he said, "shall I burn the prow? Save for that,

I dare strip no more wood from *Sun-Swan*. If I do, her frame will be left too weak to meet the rage of a storm."

"Do not burn *Sun-Swan's* prow, Lord!" cried Luf. "You will burn her luck-rune with it."

"If the rune is a rune of power," said Thorkill, "*Sun-Swan* will still be help-strong."

And to Aldi he said: "Set your axe to the prow."

So Aldi set his axe to *Sun-Swan's* swan-prow; and with it he fed the fire for a few days more. Then again he came to Thorkill.

"Lord," he said, "I have just fed the fire with the last of the prow. When that is burnt, the fire must die."

"If that is our fate," said Thorkill, "let it die."

So Aldi let the fire die. Luf stood by the fire-pit, to see the last bit of the red and gold prow burn. He saw the end of the luck-rune flare up and turn to ash. He spelt it out as it died:

> "May all things ill to you
> Turn to good-will to you!"

"An ill thing is this, Lord," he said to Thorkill, "that our strand-hew has cost us our fire. Can a thing so ill to us still turn to good-will to us?"

"If the rune is a rune of power, it can," said Thorkill.

And now the shipmen felt the full loss of the ship-fire. Gok had no fire to cook by; raw meal and raw fish was now all they had for food. Luf had no fire to light them a night-torch at; they had to grope in the dark. When they left the oar-bench, they had no fire to sit by, to thaw cold, sore hands by, to play chess or dice by, to sing songs by. Glad were they now of the bear-skin cloaks Thorkill had given them.

Prince Gotrik's red gem was all they had now to light them by night. And even by day, Thorkill was glad of its glow to see to slash each day's cut in the helm-rail.

Then, one grey day, as Thorkill stood at the helm, with Luf at his side, Luf cried:

"Lord, I see a small red star in the sky!"

Lifting his head, Thorkill saw, far off, a small red glow in the gloom. The oarsmen lay on the oars, and heads swung round to look.

"I see it, too!" — "And I!" — "And I!" they cried.

"Lord, what can it be?" asked Luf.

"It looks to me like a fire, high on a cliff-top," said Thorkill. "If this is so, we are near Fire-giant-land."

At that, a shout of joy went up from the men.

"Shall I look from the gilt-vane, Lord?" asked Luf.

"The gloom is too thick," said Thorkill. "But the red star grows so fast, I think we shall soon feel the keel grate on the strand."

They felt the keel grate on the strand. Down the ropes slid the men, and drew *Sun-Swan* up out of the sea.

"Can we get fire here, think you, Lord?" asked Aldi the Fire-Keeper.

"I go to find out," said Thorkill. "After the cost of the strand-hew, it is best that I go alone."

"It will soon be night, Lord," said Onni. "How will you find your way back to a ship that has no light?"

"Lord," cried Luf, "let me hang Prince Gotrik's arm-ring on the gilt-vane. Its red gem will show you the way."

"You counsel well, boy," said Thorkill.

And he took the ring from his own arm, and set it on Luf's. Then up the tall mast went Luf, hand over hand, and was lost in the gloom. Soon he slid down again.

"I bound the ring to the mast-head with my belt," he said, "the gem to the land. It came to me that if the gilt-vane swung, you night not see the gem, Lord."

"You did well, lad," said Thorkill. "As long as you can see, men, seek drift-wood on the strand, and stow it in the fuel-holds.

"Aldi and Luf, each bring a bar of drift-wood up the cliff to me. But till I come to you or call you, wait a stone's throw from the fire."

Then off Thorkill set in the gloom. The red star led him over the strand to the foot of a cliff. A steep track led him up. At the top he came to a cave. From the cave came the red glow he had seen as a red star.

Thorkill thrust his head into the cave. In it he saw a fire as big as a hay-rick. Round it sat three black giants.

"May I sit with you?" asked Thorkill.

The three black giants swung round to the mouth of the cave. Thorkill saw that they each had a horny nose, like a bird.

"Who spoke?" asked the first giant.

"A ship-man from lands of men," said Thorkill.

"Sit, ship-man," said the next giant.

So into the cave went Thorkill, and sat down by the fire.

"Is it far to Garfred's Treasure-Town?" he asked.

"Ship-man," said the third giant, "in this land, all things must be paid for. You must pay us first for what you wish to know."

"What will it cost?" asked Thorkill.

"A good home-truth," said the first giant. "We deal here in home-truths. Tell us the first home-truth you think of, and we will map out your way to Garfred's Treasure-Town for you."

So Thorkill told them the first home-truth that came into his head:

"Never in any home have I seen three such homely noses."

The three giants shook with giant mirth, so that three giant shadows shot up and down on the cave-wall in the fire-light.

"A good home-truth, in truth," said the next giant. "Now we will map out your way, and give you good counsel."

"Sail on North," said the third giant, "till you reach the snow-coast of Frost-giant-land. The Frost-giant Gudmund will meet your ship, and take you to his hall."

"If you do not fall into his traps," said the first giant, "he will take you to Garfred's Treasure-Town."

"What traps?" asked Thorkill.

"Let no man but the Ship-Master have speech with him," said the next giant, "and let that speech be fair speech. For the men are more apt to rash speech than the master. And rash speech can give Gudmund power to harm."

"Let no man eat of Gudmund's meat, or drink of Gudmund's wine," said the third giant, "or he will clean forget his birth-right land, and be tied for ever to Frost-giant-land."

"Let no man lay a hand on a giant maid," said the first giant, "or his wits will go from him, and never again will he be in his right mind."

"Has Treasure-Town pit-falls, too?" asked Thorkill.

"It has," said the second giant. "Giant dogs will meet you. Smear horns with fat, and fling them to the dogs to lick. Only thus can you pass in."

"Let each man take arms in with him," said the third giant. "For if one man lays a finger on any treasure, you will have sore need of arms."

"If you come forth safe from Treasure-Town," said the first giant, "ask of Gudmund the next steps of your way. As long as you do not sleep in his hall, you may trust him from then on, for he will set no more traps for you."

"You have paid me well for my home-truth," said Thorkill. "Will you add to your good counsel the gift of a live brand from your fire?"

"If you need fire," said the next giant, "you must pay for it with a new home-truth."

"Will this do?" said Thorkill. "It is wise to take good counsel, even when it is fools who give it."

Again the three giants shook with giant mirth, so that three giant shadows shot up and down on the cave-wall in the fire-light.

"A good home-truth, in truth," said the third giant. "Take your fire-brand, ship-man, and fare you well."

So Thorkill rose, and took a live brand from the fire, and gave his thanks to the three black giants. Each giant gave him a nod of his horny nose. And out from the cave went Thorkill, his firebrand in his hand.

# How Thorkill came
# to Frost-giant-land

At the mouth of the cave, Thorkill found Aldi and Luf, each with his bar of drift-wood. Thorkill lit them from his fire-brand. Then, led by Prince Gotrik's red gem at *Sun-Swan's* mast-head, they went down the steep track, each with his torch held aloft.

With a shout of joy, the shipmen ran to meet them. With the three live brands and a pile of drift-wood, they lit a fire on the strand.

Gok the Cook was glad of that fire, to broil his fish and to bake his bread. And the shipmen were glad as they smelt the rich smell for the first time for so long.

As they sat and ate, they cried to Thorkill: "Tell us how you got the fire-brand, Lord!"

And Thorkill told them.

"So along with the fire, Lord," said Aldi, "you got counsel that will stand us in good stead. Yet it was the price we had to pay for our strand-hew that sent you to beg for the fire."

"So," cried Luf, "this thing that was ill to us *did* turn to good-will to us!"

"Ah," said Bok the Store-Master, "but will it help us to know we need fat for the horns when I have not a scrap left in my foodholds?"

"Let us take turns to sleep now," said Thorkill, "and see what a new day may bring forth."

So they took turns to sleep, till the black night gave way to grey day.

Then Thorkill sent some of his men to find fresh

spring-water. Some he set to scrub deck and oar-bench with sand. And some he set to scrape the slime and the shells and the sea-weed from *Sun-Swan's* keel.

As Luf knelt at the lip of the sea, to help with this, he swung round to Thorkill.

"Lord," he said, "do mer-men swim in this sea?"

"It is too cold a sea for mer-men," said Thorkill. "Why do you ask?"

"I saw a head rise out of the water, just by the ship," said Luf. "I did not see it clear in this grey fog; but it was round, as a man's head is, with sleek black hair."

"A seal!" cried Thorkill. "It will give us the fat we lack for the horns, if we can but catch it. Sing to it, Luf. Seals love to hear men sing."

Then Luf rose, and stood at the lip of the sea, and put up his head, and sang:

> "In King Gorm's hall,
> With shields and helms and mail-coats
> The hench-men deck the wall.
> Bright, bright they gleam.
> And here grope we
> In this grey gloom,
> By this grey sea.
> Seal, seal, we need your aid!
> No more shall we see with joy
> The soft winds sweep soft spray
> Over the red and gold swan-prow.
> For *Sun-Swan* gave her swan-prow
> To feed our fire.
> *Sun-Swan* has lost her swan-prow;
> But still can her luck-rune help us,
> If you will help us.
> Seal, seal, we need your aid!

Seal, seal, this stave I sing you
To lure you to your death-doom.
We beg the boon of your life-gift,
That we may do that deed
We left our home to do.
Seal, seal, if this be your death-day,
May I, who am born a free-man,
Wear a thrall's white kirtle
If ever my song forget you!
Not till the high hills fall
Shall your fame grow old!
Seal, seal, we need your aid!"

Then, all about *Sea-Swan,* one by one, sixty sleek black heads rose out of the water. Sixty sleek black seals swam in, and lay at the lip of the sea, as still as if spellbound by Luf's song.

The men went among them with spears. They still lay as if spellbound, as if it were the will of each seal to give up his life as a free gift.

So, clean and spick-and-span, with a new fire in her fire-pit, with store of seal-meat in her food-holds, *Sun-Swan* again put out to sea.

North still she swam. The air grew chill. Frost-bind held her sails stiff, and beads of ice hung from her ropes, when she came to land at a strand white with snow.

"Now let each man bear in mind the counsel of the giants with the horny noses," said Thorkill. "And since a North-man must tell no lie, all vow with me five vows that I will tell you."

So, speaking with Thorkill, all the shipmen made the five vows:

"By *Sun-Swan's* rune of power we vow
To keep from sleep in Frost-giant-land.
By *Sun-Swan's* rune of power we vow
To bear our arms ever with us in Frost-giant-land.
By *Sun-Swan's* rune of power we vow
To drink only water till we are back in lands of men.
By *Sun-Swan's* rune of power we vow
To eat only ship-fare till we are back in lands of men.
By *Sun-Swan's* rune of power we vow
To lay no hand on a maid in dance or in revel
Till we are back in lands of men."

Then Thorkill said to Aldi the Fire-Keeper: "You, Aldi, will stay on *Sun-Swan* to keep in the ship-fire. Keep ten men with you, that *Sun-Swan* may be safe. The rest of us will go with Gudmund the Frost-giant. Each man will bear his own meat with him."

Then Gok the Cook gave to each ship-man his share of seal-meat and seal-fat to take with him.

"Each man," said Thorkill, "will bear with him his own drink."

Then Bok the Store-Master gave to each ship-man his own flask of fresh snow-water.

"Each man," said Thorkill, "will bear with him the arms he is most at home with."

Then Sild the Arms-Smith gave to each ship-man the arms he was most at home with, spear or bow or sword or sling, and a black shield or a gold shield from the side of the ship.

"Has each man his drink-horn, meat-dagger and bear-skin cloak?" asked Thorkill.

"Yes, Lord," cried the men.

"Then we are ready to meet our frost-giant host," said Thorkill. "And here, I think, he comes."

For the crunch of ice came to them out of the gloom, with a clip-clop of hooves and a cling-clang of bells.

Then out of the grey fog and over the white strand came a black bulk as big as *Sun-Swan*. As it drew near, they saw that it was a giant sledge, and that two giant beasts with giant antlers drew it.

"Never have I seen such beasts!" cried Luf. "What beasts are they, Lord?"

"They are giant rein-deer," Thorkill told him.

With a wild clash of bells, the sledge drew up by the band of shipmen. They saw a giant step out of the sledge, tall and black in the gloom. Ice hung from the bush of each eye-brow, and lay in sparks in his black beard and in the long black fur of his cap.

As he came to them, so vast was he that the shipmen drew in a sharp breath, aghast at his size.

"Have no fear, men!" said Thorkill. "The giant can do us no harm if all do as I say. Be brave. Be wary. Be silent. For King Gorm sent us forth on two quests. And we stand now on the brink of the first of them!"

# How Thorkill came
# to the Frost-giant's Hall

"I am Gudmund the Frost-giant," said the giant. "I am glad to see men again in Frost-giant-land. We see too few here. It is long since men last came to see us."

Thorkill kept in mind the counsel of the giants with the horny noses. He gave to Gudmund fair speech for his fair speech:

"We are glad to be here, Gudmund. As Ship-Master, I thank you. For my men I thank you, also."

Gudmund shot a keen eye at the throng of shipmen, each still and silent in his bear-skin cloak.

"Can your men not speak, then?" he asked.

"They have no skill in giant-speech," said Thorkill. "They have no speech but that of the land they were born in."

"What land is that?" asked Gudmund.

"Men call it Denmark," said Thorkill. "It lies most south of the lands men call the North-Lands."

"Then how came you to have skill in giant-speech?" asked Gudmund.

"My birth-right land is Iceland," Thorkill told him. "It is the land that lies most north of the lands men call the North-Lands, and so most near to Giant-land. So in Iceland men have some small skill in giant-speech."

"And the lad?" asked Gudmund, his keen eye on Luf. "Is he not from Iceland, too? To me he has the look of one with such skill in speech."

"He does have skill in speech," said Thorkill, "but not in giant-speech. He has the gift of song-craft. His birth-right land is not Iceland, but Frank-land, a land that lies to the south of Denmark."

"And why," asked Gudmund, "have you all come to Frost-giant-land from such far-off lands of men?"

"To gaze on the treasures in Garfred's Treasure-Town," said Thorkill. "Is that not in Frost-giant-land?"

"It is in Loot-giant-land," said Gudmund, "but one must cross Frost-giant-land to reach it. I will take you to it. But let us first feast, for my hall lies on the way. Bid your men get in; my sledge has room for you all."

Then Thorkill told his shipmen to get into the giant-sledge. As they got in, the bear-skin cloaks fell open, and Gudmund saw that all bore arms and drink-horns.

"You will not need arms," he said. "Bid your men hand them up to me, and I will reach and put them back on the ship for you."

"Do not take it amiss," said Thorkill, "but bear arms ever with us we must, for we are under a vow to do so."

"Then let me put back your drink-horns," said Gudmund. "Those in my hall hold far more."

"Those in your hall will be far too big for us small men to lift," said Thorkill.

When all the shipmen were in the sledge, and Thorkill with them, Gudmund got in and took up the reins. With a toss of giant antlers and a wild clash of bells, off set the giant rein-deer.

Clip-clop went the giant hoofs; cling-clang went the giant bells; crunch went the ice, as the sledge sped away, over the deep white snow of the strand, into the dark shade of a giant fir-wood.

Under the tall, dark trees sped the sledge, and out to a wide snow-plain on the far side. In the midst of this plain, the shipmen saw a vast hall loom up out of the grey gloom.

The giant sledge drew up at the vast porch of this vast hall. In at the giant door Gudmund led Thorkill and his men. As they came in, they stood in a throng, to stare about them with round eyes.

The walls of the hall rose like cliffs. So high was the roof that its beams were lost to sight. Each pine-torch that lit up the hall was as tall as a tall man.

The table by the long wall-bench was as big as King Gorm's hall. The vast vat of wine at its foot was as big as King Gorm's stable. The fires ablaze down the hall rose as high as King Gorm's roof.

Gudmund led the men to the table. As they sat down, they felt as small on that giant bench as a bird on the bench in King Gorm's hall.

Gudmund went to call his bond-maids, to wait on the men. Then Thorkill said, low and swift: "Men, drink our snow-water first. Then eat our seal-meat. Keep the seal-fat, and put it in your drink-horns. Let no man eat Gudmund's food, or drink Gudmund's drink. Let no man go to sleep. Let no man lay hand on a giant maid, or join in dance or revel."

Then back came Gudmund. With him came sixty giant bond-maids. Vast as they were, they were yet most fair of face and form.

They brought in giant drinking-horns, full to the rim of red wine. They set them on the table to tempt the men. After weeks of water, it was hard for the men to spurn such drink.

But they felt Thorkill's stern eye on them. So each

one took out his water-flask and his drink-horn, and began to take sad, slow sips of the water Bok had given them.

All save one. When he felt Thorkill's stern eye pass from him, he bent the giant wine-cup that stood near him, and let its wine flow into his mouth.

And as soon as he did this, he forgot he was a Dane. He swung this way and that, to gaze with wild eyes on his ship-mates. He began to speak a wild, new speech they did not know. When the rest saw this, glad was each of them to gulp snow-water from his own drink-horn.

Then the giant bond-maids bore dish after dish to the table, and set them down to tempt the men. Each dish was rich, both to sight and to smell. After weeks of ship-fare, it was hard for the men to spurn such food.

But they felt Thorkill's stern eye on them. So each took out his meat-dagger, and began to take sad, slow bites of the cold seal-meat Gok had given them.

All save one. When he felt Thorkill's stern eye pass from him, he put his hand into the giant dish that stood near him, and bore a rich tit-bit to his mouth.

And as soon as he did this, he forgot he was a Dane. He swung this way and that, to gaze with wild eyes on his ship-mates. He began to speak a wild, new speech they did not know.

When the rest saw this, each was glad to eat of Gok's cold seal-meat. And each took care not to eat the fat, but to put it safe in his drink-horn.

When Gudmund saw the shipmen turn from his wine and drink water, he said to Thorkill:

"Why do your men spurn my wine? To do that in Frost-giant-land is a slight upon your host."

"Take it not as such, Gudmund," said Thorkill. "We are under vow to drink only water."

When Gudmund saw the shipmen turn from each rich dish to eat cold seal-meat, he said to Thorkill:

"Why do your men spurn my feast? To do that in Frost-giant-land is a slight upon your host."

"Take it not as such Gudmund," said Thorkill. "We are under vow to eat only ship-fare."

"Such vows make my feast but a poor one," said Gudmund. "But at least the revel can be merry. See, my bond-maids wait to dance with your men."

With nods and smiles, the giant maids came to the table. Each put out a hand to grasp the hand of the ship-man next to her.

So fair in face and form were the giant maids that it was hard for the men, after weeks of toil at sea, to spurn a revel.

But they felt Thorkill's stern eye on them. So each kept his hands in his lap.

All save one. Up from the bench he got, and took a giant maid's hand in his own.

And as soon as he did this, his wits went from his, and he began to rave and to foam at the mouth like a mad dog.

When the rest saw this, each was glad to keep his own hands safe in his lap.

Then Gudmund said to Thorkill: "Why do your men spurn my maids? To do that in Frost-giant-land is a slight upon your host."

"Take it not as such, Gudmund," said Thorkill. "We are under vow not to take the hand of a maid, and not to dance or revel."

"Then let us sleep now," said Gudmund."And when we 'have slept I will take you to Garfred's Treasure-Town."

"Do not take it amiss, Gudmund," said Thorkill, "but we are under vow not to sleep till we are back at our ship. For your feast we thank you. And more still shall we thank you if you will take us now to Treasure-Town."

"Never did I meet a band of men under so many vows," said Gudmund. "Come, then."

And he led them out of the hall.

# How Thorkill came
# to Treasure-Town

At the door of the hall stood the two giant rein-deer.
Into the giant sledge got Thorkill and his men. Gudmund took up the reins.

With a toss of giant antlers, the giant rein-deer set
off. Clip-clop went the giant hooves; cling-clang went
the giant bells; crunch went the ice. Away sped the
sledge, on, on, on, on, over a snow-plain that had no
end.

Next to Thorkill, Luf gave a yawn, and his head fell
on his chest. Thorkill bent to look at him. He saw that
Luf's eyes were shut. All round him, then, he saw his
men sit, eyes shut and head on chest.

He took Luf's arm, and shook it, then bent to hiss at
his ear: "Wake up! If you sleep in this land, never
again will you wake! Shake the man next to you, and
tell him, and bid him tell the next."

Luf sat up with a jerk. He shook the man next to
him. So from man to man went hiss and pinch. And if
a head was seen to drop, still went on hiss and pinch,
till at last the sledge drew up on the bank of a wide
river.

"Frost-giant-land ends on this bank," Gudmund told
Thorkill. "Loot-giant-land lies on the far bank. I will
take you over."

By the bank was a giant raft. From giant sledge to
giant raft went Thorkill and his men. The raft was as
big as a corn-field. It had room to hold them all.

With a pine-tree for a punt-pole, Gudmund took

them over. As they drew near the other side, they saw, across the snow, grey walls loom high, as if afloat in the gloom.

"That is Treasure-Town," said Gudmund. "I will wait here for you. But why must you take so much with you? It will tire you when you have to tramp in such deep snow. Let me take care of your arms for you."

"You forget, Gudmund," said Thorkill, "that we are under vow to bear our arms ever with us."

"But not your drink-horns," said Gudmund. "At least let me take care of those."

"We may have need of them," said Thorkill.

"No, no," said Gudmund. "For if you drink of Garfred's water, you will die"

"We have our own water, if we need it," said Thorkill.

And he and his men set out to tramp across the snow to Treasure-Town.

As they drew near, they saw why from afar it had hung afloat in the grey gloom. For it stood on the top of a tall grey cliff. Steps cut in the rock led up to it.

At the foot of the steps stood giant dogs, each as big as an ox. They began to prowl and to bark and growl as the men drew near

"Let each man fling down his drink-horn," cried Thorkill.

Each man flung down his drink-horn on the snow. The giant dogs sprang at the drink-horns, and began to lick out the seal-fat. They paid no more heed to the men.

Swift up the steps went Thorkill. Swift up the steps went his shipmen, four by four. At the top of the steps a giant gate stood open. Into Treasure-Town they went.

No sound came to them from the street, as wide and as bare as a river. No sound came to them from the walls, as tall as cliffs. In the grey gloom all was still , as if all in the town were dead.

Along the wide street went Thorkill and his men. Not a door, not a porch, did they see, till they came to a giant hall.

Each stone in its walls was a rock as big as King Gorm's porch. The roof of the hall was lost in the gloom; but they saw that the roof of the porch had giant spear-heads, set up on end, to thatch it. The open doorway was vast and dark.

"This must be Garfred's Treasure-Hall," said Thorkill. "Let us go in.

But some of the men shrank back.

Then said Thorkill: "Men, we have come far to see this marvel. Do not let fear rob you of it now that, after many pains, it is in your grasp. Now who goes in with me?"

"I, Lord," cried Luf.

"And I," cried Sild the Arms-Smith.

"My brother and I," cried Bok and Gok.

"My brother and I," cried Onni and Omd.

"And I, and I," cried the rest.

"You have seen," said Thorkill, "how we have lost three good men who forgot the counsel of the horny noses. Do not forget that counsel now. Gaze your fill; but lay no finger on any thing in this hall. If you do this, no harm will come to us. If you fail to do this, you bring down dread doom on us all. Now let us go in, four by four."

So, four by four, all went in.

Beyond the porch-door was an inner door. When Thorkill threw this open, the men stood still to blink, so bright was the light that met them. It was as if the sun had left the sky to dwell in that hall.

Floor, door, walls, roof, all were of gold. The men trod on gold. The glow from the gold room beat down on them. Along the walls lay gold in heaps, in banks, in hills.

On each hill of gold lay a giant, club in hand. They lay so still that Luf asked: "Are they dead?"

"No," said Thorkill. "But in so deep a sleep are they sunk that as long as we only gaze, they will not wake."

And when Luf came near to them across that giant hall, he saw that each giant chest rose and fell, and that the beard of each giant flew up with each breath he took in, and blew back with each breath he let out.

Fingers began to itch at the sight of so much gold.

"Let no man lift a finger," cried Thorkill, "to lay it on that gold!"

At the far end of the hall, a door led to a second hall. This hall was lit as if by fire.

Floor, door, walls, roof, all were of gems. The men trod on gems. The flash of gems in the roof beat down on them, red, green, white, blue. Along the walls lay gems in heaps, in banks, in hills.

Fingers began to itch at the sight of so many gems.

"Let no man lift a finger," cried Thorkill, "to lay it on a gem!"

At the far end of the hall of gems, a door led to a third hall. In the midst of this hall was a high-seat, as big as a boat. In it sat a giant, clad in cloth-of-gold.

He slept, like all the rest.

"This must be Garfred," said Thorkill.

By the high-seat stood seven vast wine-casks, each as big as a hill. Gold ran in heaps round them. The staves of wood had begun to rot, and out of the chinks spilt such treasure as few men had ever seen — belts of gems, head-bands of gems, crowns set thick with gems, swords of gold with hilts of gems, spears of gold with gems for spear-heads.

On Garfred's giant arm was a giant arm-ring. It was as thick as a man's arm, made of gold in the form of a snake, with two red gems for eyes."

In Garfred's hand was a giant stag-horn, of gold, set thick with gems.

By Garfred's side stood a mammoth tusk, laid all over with gold.

Its tip was set in the floor. Out of its high brim, red wine shot up to the roof and fell back into the tusk.

Fingers began to itch at the sight of so much treasure.

"Let no man lift a finger," cried Thorkill, "to lay it on anything here!"

But three men broke forth from the ranks.

The first set greedy hands on Garfred's arm-ring. As he tore it off, it slid, a live thing, from his hands. In and out among the men its dread head shot; in and out of its dread mouth shot its dread venom-fork.

As the second man tore the giant stag-horn from Garfred's grasp, it began to twist and to turn. It began to dart to and fro, and to gore the men all about it.

The third man tried to tip the mammoth tusk, that he might drink its wine. Crash, it fell; and out began to pour the wine in a swift red river. The red flood rose till it was so deep that the men must swim or sink.

And at that crash, the giants woke.

Up they rose, with shouts of rage. From all four walls of all three halls they strode, with clubs held high.

As Thorkill gave his war-cry, the flame died out of

the gems, the light died out in the gold. As black as pitch now were the three vast halls.

How glad was each man now that he bore his arms under his cloak! How good it felt to grip the hilt of a true sword, to let spear fly, to cast dart, to twang bow, to fit stone to sling!

With splash and clash, with slip and slide and glide, the shipmen swam to the rim of the wine-flood. Thorkill led them out from among the legs of his giant foes. Yet with each step they took, a man fell.

Left in the dark, the giants fell on each other.

From the third hall to the second, from the second to the first, fled the men. And when at last they found the porch-door, how good it was to pass out of that loud black gloom into the silent grey gloom of the town!

Along the wide grey street they ran. Down the steep grey steps they fell. Past the giant-dogs and the drink-horns they shot like stones from a sling.

Not till they were out in the midst of the snow did they stop.

Then Thorkill held a roll-call.

Luf and Sild, Onni and Omd, Gok and Bok were all safe. But of the rest of the men who went into Treasure-Town with Thorkill, only one in four came out.

# How Thorkill came
# to the Giant-god's land

So back over the deep snow to the river went Thorkill, with all that was left of his men.

Gudmund still sat on his giant raft, just as they had left him. But, just as the horny noses had said, from now on, no more traps did he set for them.

Over the river he took them, to his sledge on the far bank. Each man now had all too much room on the giant raft, and on the giant sledge.

Swift as the wind went the giant rein-deer over the wide snow-plain. Swift as the wind they drew the sledge past the black bulk of Gudmund's hall. Swift as the wind the sledge bore all that was left of the ship-men into the dark fir-wood, and out to the white strand on the other side.

It was good then to see the red glow of the gem at *Sun-Swan's* mast-head. It was good to hear Aldi's men hail them with joy as the sledge drew up by the ship.

"The thanks of us all to you, Gudmund," said Thorkill. "With your help, and at some cost, we have seen such a marvel as King Gorm's eyes will shine to hear of."

"Do you sail back to him now?" asked Gudmund.

"First I must seek out the Giant-God, Utgard-Loki," said Thorkill.

"Then you must still sail North," Gudmund told him, "till the tide casts you up on a black strand, rocks from end to end. This is the Land of Utgard. In it, Utgard-Loki dwells."

"How shall we find his abode?" asked Thorkill.

"From end to end of the strand you will find but one track," said Gudmund. "And that track will take you to him."

"Do men bear arms when they seek out a god?" asked Thorkill.

"No," said Gudmund. "But let each man take a live firebrand in his hand, and on his arm an ox-hide."

"That counsel has an odd ring," said Thorkill. "But we thank you for it, Gudmund."

"I can give you more," said Gudmund, "if you will tell me what your name means in the speech of man."

"Thorkill means *Hench-man to Thor*," Thorkill told him.

"Then," said Gudmund, "when you get back to the lands of men, *if* you get back to the lands of men, give heed to the news the Shaven Man will give you at Thor's Oak."

"Never did I hear of a Shaven Man," said Thorkill, "but Thor's Oaks in the North-Lands are many. How shall I seek out the right one?"

"As to that," said Gudmund, "Fate will lend a hand."

Then he sat in his sledge, and took up the reins. A toss of giant antlers, a clip-clop of giant hooves, a cling-clang of giant bells, a crunch of ice, and soon he was lost in the gloom.

Then Thorkill said to Luf: "Bid Gok cook the men hot food, and then let them sleep."

When the shipmen had fed well and slept well, Thorkill said to Bok the Store-Master: "Bid the men pack tight all the water-skins with snow, and fuel the fuel-holds with fuel from the fir-wood."

This the men did.

"And now let us sail," said Thorkill.

So the men slid *Sun-Swan* into the sea; and she swam North in the gloom.

It was hard for so few men to row *Sun-Swan* now, and there was more room on her oar-seats than men to fill it.

The drift of the sea now grew cold; the air cut like a sword-edge. The sails hung as stiff as planks. The men's hands froze as they tried to claw at the oars. Hail smote them like storms of stones cast down from the sky. Ears were a-scorch with frostbite. Snow drove in gusts of white stings across the grey gloom.

And now it was not grey gloom, but black gloom. In that black gloom, on and on to the North swam *Sun-Swan*. In that black gloom, she came at last to the Land of Utgard. In that black gloom, the tide cast her up on its black strand. In that black gloom, the men drew her up on its beach.

Luf asked Thorkill, aghast: "Lord, can this in truth be the home-land of a god? Why must he dwell in so wild and so dark a place?"

"Ah, why? I, too, ask why," said Thorkill.

In his mind's eye he saw bright Frey, with his fields of gold corn. In his mind's eye he saw bright Baldur, with his gold sun. He shook his head.

"It may be when we see him, we shall know," he said. "Luf, bid Onni and Omd take six men, to seek out the track on the strand. And bid Aldi give them a fire-brand each, to seek with."

From end to end of the strand went Onni and Omd and the six men, each with his red fire-brand a-flame in the black gloom. Then back to *Sun-Swan* they came.

"Lord," said Onni, "only one track can we find."

"That is as Gudmund told me," said Thorkill. "Aldi will stay, to keep in the ship-fire, and five men with him. Bok, give the rest of the men an ox-hide each from your store."

"Lord," said Bok the Store-Master, "I have no such things in my store."

"But *Sun-Swan* has, Lord," cried Luf. "We can take down the oxhide roof that keeps the spray from the deck. If we cut the thongs, it will fall apart, and each man can have an ox-hide."

"This will we do," said Thorkill.

And, by the light of fire-brands held by some of the men, this the rest of them did.

Then said Thorkill to Aldi: "Give each man a live brand from the ship-fire."

And this Aldi did.

Then each man took his fire-brand in his hand, and his oxhide on his arm. And Thorkill took also the rich cup King Gorm had given him to take to Utgard-Loki as a gift. Onni and Omd led Thorkill to the track. And they all set out along it in a torchlit file.

By the light of his own brand, Thorkill saw black rocks loom up on all sides. Not a blade of grass, not a leaf, not a bud, not a bit of moss, not a green thing of any kind was to be seen.

The track went in and out along the bare black rocks. From black strand it led up to steep black cliffs. Up the steep track they went till it came to an end. It went into a black hole in the side of the black cliff.

Then Thorkill stood still, to gaze at that black hole with dread.

And all his men stood still, to gaze with dread with him.

"How can a black hole be the doorway of a god, Lord?" asked Luf, aghast.

"Ah, how? I, too, ask how," said Thorkill.

In his mind's eye, he saw the halls of the good gods of Asgard, as the glee-men in Iceland sang of them.

They had walls of silver, and roofs of gold, and door-posts made of gems. They had no need of any pine-brand torch. For a light more bright than day-light came from the god on the high-seat.

"Can this be the right track, Lord?" asked Luf.

"From end to end of the strand did we seek," said Onni, "and this is the only one."

"I like this quest the less, the more I see of it," said Thorkill. "Yet so far have we come, we must go on now to its end."

And he held his torch high, and led his men into the black hole in the black cliff.

# How Thorkill came
# to the Giant-god

When Thorkill led his men into the black hole in the black cliff, it grew less and less in size till they came to two doorposts of black rock. So low was the roof of this doorway that the men had to drop to hands and knees to creep in.

They crept into a black cave. Its roof of black rock was low, but not as low as the doorway. Its walls of black rock were full of holes and chinks and rents.

It was a place to chill the blood.

As the fire-brands lit the floor of the cave, Thorkill saw that it was deep in mud and mire.

As the fire-brands lit the roof of the cave, he saw that it was thick with black bats. They slept as they hung from it, heads down, wings laid back.

As the fire-brands lit the walls of the cave, Thorkill saw that it was thick with black snakes. They, too, slept, in tight coils like springs, in the holes and chinks and rents in the black rock.

On in the mud and mire went Thorkill and his men, each with fire-brand held to help him pick his way. They came to a slow black stream that crept across the cave. When they tried to wade it, they found it was a stream, not of water, but of thick mud. From the depths of the cave beyond it came a sound like far-off thunder.

Thick with mud from foot to hip, they came to the far side of the stream. The floor of the cave, as they went on, began to slope at a down-tilt. From the far end of the cave, a foul smell blew to meet them.

Now the far-off thunder was not so far-off; now it grew near. The slope of the ground, slight at first, grew more and more steep. They stood at last at the edge of a deep pit.

The hair of each man rose on end. For in that deep pit sat a giant, more vast in size than even Gudmund or Garfred. His head stood out from the top of the pit. The rest of him was lost in the black gloom below.

His eye-lids, as big as wine-cups, were fast shut. He, too, slept, like the black bats and the black snakes. As he drew it in and blew it out, his breath made a wind in the cave. Each snore was a loud clap of thunder.

Thorkill held his fire-brand low, to peer into the pit. He saw that the giant's giant hands were held fast in thick bonds of lead, like hand-cuffs. Deep, deep in the pit, he saw the dull glint of bonds of lead that held fast his legs and his feet.

Such a reek came from the hairs on the giant's chin that Thorkill held his breath. Each hair on that vast chin was as long as a spear, and as stiff as a spear.

"Who can this foul giant be?" asked Sild the Arms-Smith, with a gasp.

Next to him, Luf held his fire-brand high. It lit up a vast crown of lead on the giant's vast bald head.

"Look, Lord!" he cried. "His crown has a rune on it!"

"All hold your brands high," said Thorkill, "to give me light to read this rune."

Then, at the rim of that pit, each ship-man held his

torch high. As the red light swung to and fro on the crown, Thorkill saw the rune that ran round it.

He spelt it out: "Utgard-Loki."

"Utgard-Loki?" cried Luf. He stood on tip-toe, to peer at the rune. "Yes, Lord, you are right. Utgard-Loki."

"Utgard-Loki?" cried the throng of men, aghast.

"Can this foul giant be King Gorm's god?" cried Thorkill. "Is this the god we have been sent so far, and at such cost in pain and men, to ask of things too deep for the wit of man? Yet must I ask what I was sent to ask, and give what I was sent to give. Yet how can I wake him?"

"Call him by name, Lord," said Luf.

So Thorkill cried, as loud as he was able: "Utgard-Loki!"

The name ran down into the pit. The name ran back along the low roof of the cave. The name ran round and round the ring-wall of the cave. It grew to a roar as loud as the giant's snore. It died away.

But still Utgard-Loki slept.

Then Thorkill said to Luf: "Luf, call him by name with me."

So Luf and Thorkill cried, as loud as both were able: "Utgard-Loki!"

Again the name ran down into the pit, and back along the low roof, and round and round the ring-wall of the cave. Again it grew to a roar as loud as the giant's snore. Again it died away.

But still Utgard-Loki slept.

Then Thorkill said to the throng of men: "Men, all call him by name with me."

Then all the men cried with Thorkill, as loud as they were able: "Utgard-Loki!"

So loud was the shout that the name broke on them like a clap of thunder. It grew to a roar. It died away.

But still Utgard-Loki slept.

Then Luf said to Thorkill: "Lord, when I was small, if my father slept too long, it was my joy to pluck a hair from his chin to wake him. Never did this fail. Shall I wake this giant-god thus?"

"It is an odd way to wake a god," said Thorkill, "but do it, boy."

Then Luf gave his fire-brand to Sild, who stood next to him, and set both his hands to a hair in the giant's chin. He began to tug at it. He began to strain at it. But to pluck it out he was not able. It did not even bend.

And still Utgard-Loki slept.

"Help me, Sild!" cried Luf.

So Sild gave his own fire-brand to Gok to hold, and Luf's he gave to Bok. He set his strong smith's arms about Luf; and again Luf set both his hands to the hair in the giant's chin.

Luf began to tug and to strain at the hair. Sild began to tug and to strain at Luf. But still they were not able to pluck out the hair. Still it did not even bend.

And still Utgard-Loki slept.

"Help us, Gok!" cried Sild.

So Gok gave his own fire-brand to Onni to hold, and Sild's he gave to Omd. He set his strong cook's arms about Sild. Sild set his strong smith's arms about Luf; and again Luf set both his hands to the hair in the giant's chin.

Luf began to tug and to strain at the hair. Sild began to tug and to strain at Luf. Gok began to tug and to strain at Sild.

And, this time, out with a jerk came the hair, as long and as stiff as a spear.

But still Utgard-Loki slept.

But not so the rest of the cave. At that shock it sprang into life.

With a clap of thunder seven times as loud as the giant's snore, the roof of the cave began to rock, and the walls began to reel.

The clap of thunder woke the black bats that hung from the roof. They spread black webs of wings. They flew at the shipmen. The black wings beat about each face. The hooks of feet they had hung by tried to catch and scratch each man's eyes.

The clap of thunder woke the black snakes that slept in the walls. Each tight coil sprang out like a spring set free. Each mouth flew wide, to drip venom with each hiss.

"Up with your ox-hides, men," cried Thorkill. "And back to the ship!"

Each man slid under his ox-hide. In its lee each man held his fire-brand, to keep it lit. Luf took his own from Bok; Gok took his from Onni; Sild took his from Omd.

Then back ran all the shipmen up the long, steep slope from the rim of the pit. Across the stream of mud they went. Along the rest of the cave they ran, to the tight, low door-posts of black rock.

On the ox-hides fell venom, thick and fast, like rain. With strong-wings the black bats tried to beat the ox-hides aside. With strong foot-hooks they tried to rend them.

In at a rent made thus in Onni's ox-hide came a drop of venom, and fell on his right eye. It lost its sight as he ran.

The bats beat down the left side of Omd's ox-hide, so

that a drop of venom fell on his left arm. It grew into a dry stick as he ran.

Out from the black door-posts crept the men, as fast as might be, head to heel. Out from the black hole they ran.

It was as black out as in. Sleet like spears met them. The chill winds cut like swords.

Yet sweet to them all was that free air. Good to them all did it feel to set foot on the track that led down to the strand. And best of all was it to see the red glow of Prince Gotrik's gem at *Sun-Swan's* mast-head.

# How Thorkill came to Frank-land

As they ran down the torch-lit track, Luf cried to Thor-kill: "Lord, what will you do with King Gorm's gift-cup?"

For by the light of his fire-brand he saw that Thor-kill still bore the cup King Gorm had sent to Utgard-Loki.

"I will take it back to King Gorm, boy," said Thorkill. "And what will you do with that spear with its vile reek?"

For by the light of his fire-brand he saw that Luf still bore the hair from the giant's chin.

"I will take it back to King Gorm, Lord," said Luf, with a grin.

"It is all we *shall* take back from Utgard-Loki," said Thorkill. "No news do we take back, to meet the old king's need, of an abode of the gods such as he will be glad to go to."

"We are not yet home, Lord," said Luf. "We still may meet with good news on the way."

"Then let us go to meet it," said Thorkill. "Men, let us sail!"

Some of the men held fire-brands high, to light the black gloom, and the rest gave a long push, a strong push, to slide *Sun-Swan* into the sea.

But *Sun-Swan* lay still at the lip of the sea.

"She stands as fast," cried Sild, "as if an ice-pack held her."

"An ice-pack it is!" cried Luf.

For as he held out his fire-brand, he saw that the lip

of the sea was one long sheet of ice. The sides of the ship were thick with ice. The oars were held fast by ice. The ropes were ropes of ice. A rim of ice lay round each shield.

A gasp of fear went up from all the shipmen as each held his fire-brand near to look.

"Lords," said Sild, "from such bonds no man can get *Sun-Swan* free."

"In such a plight," said Aldi, "only a god can help us."

"But what god can we ask to help us?" cried Onni, and he put up his hand to his blind eye. "The gods of old were full of care for man. But since the Dusk, they are no more at man's side."

"Only Utgard-Loki is left. And now that we have seen him, think you we can get help from *him?*" cried Omd, with a lift of the dry stick that had been his arm.

"Lord," said Luf to Thorkill, "you told at King Gorm's table of a God who is still to come."

"You are right, boy," said Thorkill. "Only the God who is to come is left to man now."

And he stood up with his face to the East. And he began to chant:

> "Give us, O King of the Winds' Hall,
> The wind that we need.
> May the Lord of the Earth and the Sun's Tent
> Hold his hand over me.
> May the God who has still care for all things
> Melt the ice of our bonds.
> May the Maker of Gem-Lea bring *Sun-Swan*
> Safe to sun-blest lands of men."

And as he did so, the ice-pack began to crack. With a sound like a clap of thunder, the ice-floes drew apart.

They left a lane of water. Into it *Sun-Swan* slid.

A wind sprang up. It thrust *Sun-Swan* along this lane, and out into the open sea.

In the black gloom, Thorkill stood at the helm, and Luf stood at his side.

"Blow, blow, kind wind!" sang Luf.

And the kind wind blew. South it blew *Sun-Swan*, out of black gloom into grey gloom.

South it blew her still, past the snow-bound strand of Frost-giant-land.

And still it blew her south, past Fire-giant-land, with the cave-fire of the horny noses a red star high in the grey gloom.

And still south it blew her, past the strand of the shipmen's strand-hew, and the green fields of Herd-giant-land, dim in the grey gloom.

"Blow, blow, kind wind!" sang Luf.

Still south the kind wind blew the ship, till she came to the tall cliffs of water that stood as still as stone in the grey gloom.

With rip of foam, the sea-walls fell. Over the heads of the shipmen, they broke in a wave with tips of fire. Then out on the other side of the sea-walls the kind wind blew the ship, into the Sea that Rings the Earth.

"Blow, blow, kind wind!" sang Luf.

And now, with joy, the shipmen saw the grey gloom grow thin, till soon it was just a pale mist.

Still south the kind wind blew the ship. And now it was to all the shipmen as if *Sun-Swan* swam out of a dark dream, and again the way lay open into the life of men.

For now, as night came on, and the sky grew black, they saw a soft white gleam far south over the sea.

"What is it, Lord?" asked Luf.

"It is our first sight of the moon," said Thorkill.

Then Luf stood up, and sang the first stave of a new oar-song:

> "Over the sea, far south, I see a gleam,
> The soft white track of the moon-way,
> The first white light to bless us
> For many a long, dark day.
> Blow, blow, kind wind!
> Soon, new to our gloom-blind eyes,
> Will the brave red sun wake up the sky.
> Ah, best of all to me!"

And so it was. Under the white moon-way, *Sun-Swan* swam past the dark mass of Iceland on the sky-line to the West. When her first dawn broke, Norway lay to the East, and it was over its hilltops the shipmen saw the first red flush of sunrise.

Then Luf stood by the helm, and sang new staves of his new oar-song:

> "I see in the East a line of land,
> Of all the sun-blest lands of men
> The first to bless our eyes.
> Blow, blow, kind wind!
> Faint spears of light
> Flash up from its dark hill-tops.
> See how the good light flowers,
> Till all Earth's roof burns gold.
> Hail, ship-mates, our first dawn!
> Ah, best of all to me!
>
> Sweet, after giant gloom, to see
> The white swell of smooth wave-crests.

Sweet to see sun and star,
Bright day, and smile of ship-mate.
Blow, blow, kind wind!
Soon now shall I see my birth-strand.
Dear is the land I look for —
Ah, best of all to me!"

And still south the kind wind blew *Sun-Swan,* all down the long, zig-zag coast of Norway.

And still south the kind wind blew her, past King Gorm's haven, past all the strands of Denmark.

In the red light of sunset, it blew her to land at last, in a haven new to Thorkill.

"Lord," cried Luf, "it is, it is my own birth-strand! Do you call to mind the song I sang to tell you all I knew of ship-craft? How I told of the boat that was my name-gift, and how it swam home to my father's haven? This, Lord, is that haven!"

"Thanks for this safe landfall," said Thorkill, "to the God who is still to come."

Then to Luf he said: "Up to the mast-head for the last time, boy, and bring me down my arm-ring."

So up went Luf to the mast-head, hand over hand; and down he slid with Prince Gotrik's arm-ring. Thorkill took it, and set it on his own arm.

Then the shipmen drew up *Sun-Swan* on the strand. And home to his father's hall Luf took Thorkill and all his band.

# How Thorkill came to Thor's Oak

Loud rang that hall with mirth that night. Full of joy was Luf's father to see his son, and proud to hear Thorkill speak so well of him.

Rich was the feast. It felt good to Thorkill and his shipmen to sit again on a bench by the shield-hung wall of a lord's hall. It felt good to eat and drink again at a still table. Good it was, too, to think of sleep in a still land-bed when it was time to go to rest.

As the thralls ran to and fro with dish and wine-cup, Luf asked: "What news is new in Frank-land, my father?"

"The news most new," said his father, with a smile, "is your own and *Sun-Swan's* landfall. And next to that is the news of the Shaven Man at Thor's Oak."

"The Shaven Man at Thor's Oak?" cried Thorkill. "Then this will be he that Gudmund the Frost-Giant told of. *Give heed,* said he, *to the news the Shaven Man will give you at Thor's Oak.* Is it known what news he brings?"

"His news," Luf's father told him, "is of a new God who is come to men."

"Now do I know," cried Thorkill, "why our kind wind blew us past King Gorm's haven to this Frankish landfall. For when I asked of Gudmund, *How shall I seek out the right Thor's Oak?* he told me, *As to that, Fate will lend a hand.* How far is this Thor's Oak?"

"You can ride to it and back in a day," Luf's father told him. "I will lend you a steed, and Luf shall show you the way. But now it is time to go to rest. May you sleep well, this first night on land in a landsman's bed!"

And so they did.

Next day, at sunrise, all were up, and Thorkill said to Luf's father: "If I stay to go to Thor's Oak, then I must send a man to King Gorm, to tell him of *Sun-Swan's* safe landfall."

"I will lend him a steed," said Luf's father.

Then Thorkill chose Aldi the Fire-Keeper to ride to King Gorm.

"Tell King Gorm," said Thorkill, "that *Sun-Swan* is back from Giant-land, and will soon swim into his haven. But keep the tale of our quests for me to tell him in full when I come."

"And if men press for this tale, Lord?" Aldi asked him.

"Then you will tell them," said Thorkill, "how you were left on *Sun-Swan* to keep in the ship-fire, and so did not go to Treasure Town or Utgard-Loki. This is why I send *you*, Aldi. For King Gorm will find our news such dread news that I fear for his life if he hears it told in too harsh a way."

Then off rode Aldi; and the rest of the shipmen Thorkill sent down to the strand, to put *Sun-Swan* ship-shape.

But Onni and Omd came to Thorkill, and said: "Lord, may we two go with you to Thor's Oak? For never again will we two bend knee to King Gorm's god, who has torn an eye and an arm from us. Much, then, do we long to hear this Shaven Man's news of the new God who is come."

"Ride with us you shall," said Thorkill, "if Luf can get steeds for you."

This Luf did. Then, his new spear in his hand, he

rode ahead and led Thorkill and Onni and Omd over the hills to Thor's Oak.

It was noon when at last Luf drew rein at the brow of a hill, and told Thorkill: "Below, Lord, stands Thor's Oak."

Thorkill and Onni and Omd drew rein, to gaze at the plain below.

From end to end the plain below was a mass of men. All stood to face a vast oak-tree.

From the hill, Thorkill saw only its zig-zag twigs, that spread out far and wide. But as he rode down, he saw that its trunk was stout and tall, and that it was as big an oak as he had ever seen in any of the lands of men.

As they drew near, from under the oak came the sound of a harp, and of a song that was sung to it. The sound of that harp and that song made Thorkill start. His long, lean face lit up.

"It is one of the old lays of Iceland," he cried. "It is the song I told King Gorm of, that tells of the Dusk of the God's and of the new God who is to come."

And on he rode, full of joy. And Luf and Onni and Omd rode on with him.

At the edge of the throng they drew rein. Over the heads of the men, they saw that a stone cross had been set up under Thor's Oak. Three steep stone steps led up to the cross.

They saw that on the top step sat a man, his harp on his knee, his hands on the strings of his harp. It was this man who sang.

He was as long and as lean as Thorkill. The front of his head was bare of hair from ear to ear. His face was thin. His eyes were like two fire-brands in his head.

Never had Thorkill seen a man clad as this man was

clad. He wore a long black kirtle, girt with a black rope. On his back hung a black hood. His feet were bare.

And that vast throng of Franks stood spellbound as he sang:

> "The sea shall rise
> In storms to the stars.
> Fire shall lick the land.
> From the skies shall sweep
> Grim gales of snow and bitter blasts.
> But then shall come
> A King among gods.
> His name I dare not
> Yet make known.
> Dim grow men's eyes
> At the Dusk of the Gods.
> Few eyes can see
> Beyond that Dusk.
> But mine can see
> Things yet to come.
> A hall I see.
> More fair than the sun
> Is this hall of gems,
> With its roof of gold.
> In Gem-Lea shall dwell
> All things that are good,
> Blest with all joy,
> To the end of all Time."

At the end of his song, the man lay down his harp. He rose. He stood, long and lean, on the top step of the cross.

He began to speak: "The old gods of Asgard were good. Did not Odin give his eye to win speech for man?"

"He did!" cried the throng of Franks.

"Did not Frey make the corn grow for man?" the Shaven Man went on.

"He did!" cried the throng of Franks.

"Was not Thor with his hammer ever man's helper?" asked the Shaven Man.

"He was!" cried the throng of Franks.

"Was not Baldur fair and kind?" asked the Shaven Man.

"He was!" cried the throng of Franks.

"But then came the Dusk of the Gods," the Shaven Man went on. "It hid the good gods of Asgard from men's sight. And who are left?"

"The giant-gods!" cried the throng of Franks.

"And are the giant-gods good?" asked the Shaven Man. "Do they help man? Are they full of care for man, as the gods of Asgard were? No! They have led men to take ill ways, dark ways. And even they sleep now. They sleep in pits, with bonds of lead on hand and foot, amid bats and snakes, in foul caves in black night!"

"But not so Utgard-Loki!" cried some of the Franks. "Do not dare, Shaven One, to speak thus of Utgard-Loki!"

And they took up stones, to stone him.

Then Thorkill cried out, and his shout rang out over the throng: "This Shaven One speaks truth, Franks. My men and I saw it with our own eyes! Make way, and we will show you!"

Then the throng of Franks made a lane, and along it rode Thorkill, with Luf and Onni and Omd, to the foot of the cross. At the side of the Shaven Man, Thorkill swung round his steed to face the Franks. And he told them all that he and his shipmen saw and did in the cave of Utgard-Loki.

"Onni, stand forth!" cried Thorkill.

And Onni rode out to Thorkill's side, that the Franks might see his venom-blind eye.

"Omd, stand forth!" cried Thorkill.

And Omd rode out to Onni's side, that the Franks might see his venom-dry arm.

"Luf, stand forth!" cried Thorkill.

And Luf rode forth, and held up the hair from the giant's chin that the Franks might see it.

"It is Luf! It is the little Lord Luf!" cried the Franks. "The Shaven Man speaks truth, for our own lordling saw it!"

Then the Shaven Man began to speak again. He spoke of the King among gods that the old lays told of, the God still full of care for man, the God who was yet to come.

"Well has Thor's Oak a new name!" he cried. "Well do men call it now Gospel Oak, the Oak of Good News! For under Thor's Oak I bring you good news, Franks: *this God is now come!*"

"Does the Shaven One still speak the truth, little Lord Luf?" asked the Franks. "Have *you* seen this new God's care for man?"

"I have," cried Luf.

And he told them how Thorkill had asked help of this God when *Sun-Swan* was ice-fast, and how the ice split and a kind wind blew them south all the long way from Giant-land to Frank-land.

"Then this new God shall be our God," cried the Franks. "Tell us more, Shaven One!"

And the Shaven Man told them more.

When he came to an end, Thorkill said to him:"I have still to take my news of Utgard-Loki to the king who sent me for it. But when I have told him my news, I will come back to you!"

# How Thorkill came back
# to Denmark

Swift was the steed Luf's father had lent to Aldi the Fire-Keeper. Soon Aldi came out of Frank-land into Denmark and King Gorm's hall.

King Gorm the Old sat at table, with his hench-men and his bench-men, when the horn blew at the gate. At King Gorm's nod, the door-ward drew back the door-bar, and into the hall came Aldi.

"It is Aldi! It is Aldi, back from Giant-land!" cried each man to the next.

Aldi came up the hall. He stood before King Gorm the Old on his high-seat.

"Lord," he said, "Lord Thorkill sends me to say he will soon be with you."

The old king's dull old eyes lit up.

"He is safe?" he asked.

"He is safe, Lord," said Aldi. "Sun-Swan reached harbour safely, but in Frank-land. That is why he sends me ahead."

"Did he gaze on Garfred's treasure?" asked the old king."Did he find my god, Utgard-Loki?"

"Lord, he did both," said Aldi. "But it is his wish to let the full tale wait, for him to tell it."

"Thorkill is right," said King Gorm. "Such a tale gains much if told by its own hero."

And he asked no more of Aldi.

Down the long table flew the news: "Thorkill did what he went to do! He saw Garfred's treasure. He found Utgard-Loki! And soon he will be back!"

Prince Gotrik's face was bright with joy at the news. All down the long table, face after face grew bright with joy at the news.

But the faces of the five lords of the Fima-Feng grew long and dark at the news. The five lords drew into a bunch, like the fingers of a hand all set to snatch.

"Thorkill must have nine lives, like a cat," said Long-Man, "to come back safe from Giant-land!"

"Look at King Gorm," said Lick-Pot, "all agog to see him!"

"By hook or by crook," said Ring-Man, "we must get him *not* to see him."

"But how can we bend his will to ours?" asked Little-Man.

"Let us see if Aldi can help us," said Thumb.

When the meal was over, and the king and his men sat at wine, Aldi went up and down the bench, to greet his old bench-mates, and to drink with all in turn.

When they saw the flush of too much wine on Aldi's face, the five lords sent to bid him come and drink with them.

They set in his hand a fine ale-horn, bound with silver. When they had drunk with him, Long-Man said: "Keep the horn as a gift, Aldi. And tell us what you saw in Treasure-Town and in the abode of Utgard-Loki."

"Not a thing did I see, Lord," said Aldi. "I had the shipfire to keep in, so I did not go to Treasure-Town, nor yet to Utgard-Loki's cave."

"Cave?" cried Lick-Pot. "Can our king's god dwell in a cave? Such news will be a shock to him."

But now Aldi was too drunk for wisdom.

"That is why Lord Thorkill bids me let the full tale wait for *him* to tell," he said. "For so dread is his news that he fears for the king's life when he hears it."

When Aldi went from them, the five lords gave each other a nod and a wink and a sin-sly grin.

That night the five lords lit the old king to his rest. Torch in hand, they stood silent by his bed. The face of each was long and sad.

"What ails you all," asked King Gorm, "that you look as if your doom drew near?"

Long-Man shook his head, and gave a sigh.

"Lord," he said, "it is *your* doom we see draw near."

"How so?" asked King Gorm, with a start.

"Lord," said Lick-Pot, "well is it known that it needs but a shock to kill the old and weak. That is why we fear for our dear lord."

"But what shock is this you fear for me?" asked the old king.

"The shock of Thorkill's news, Lord," said Ring-Man. "For we have found out from Aldi that so dread is the news Thorkill brings, he has but to tell it to our dear lord, to bring his death-hour on him."

"I see but one way for our dear lord to save his life," said Little-Man.

"What way is that?" asked the old king.

"Lord, not to let Thorkill tell you his news," said Little-Man.

"You are right," said the old king. "I will not let Thorkill tell me his news."

"I see but one way for our dear lord not to let Thorkill tell him his news," said Thumb.

"What way is that?" asked the old king.

"Lord, not to see Thorkill at all," said Thumb.

"You are right," said the old king, his face white with fear. "I will not see Thorkill at all."

And next day he set a door-ward in the porch of the hall, spear in hand, to bar the way when Thorkill came.

And that same night, Thorkill came.

For when Thorkill rode back from Thor's Oak to the hall of Luf's father, the creak of the wind-vane met his ears.

"Lord," said Luf, "our kind wind veers right round. It is set fair now to blow us to King Gorm's haven."

"Then if *Sun-Swan* is ship-shape," said Thorkill, "let us sail."

"Lord," said Sild the Arms-Smith, "we have still much to do to her. For her frame is weak from the loss of so much wood; and we shall need to tar her seams and give her new paint and mend her sails if she is to make a brave show as she swims into King Gorm's haven."

"It is not far," said Thorkill, "and if we sail now, we have a brisk wind to help us. We will hug the coast; she will have no storms to face. And her sea-scars we can be proud of. So let us sail now."

And sail then they did.

So it was dusk when *Sun-Swan* came home to King Gorm's haven, with no prow and no ox-hide deck-roof, her planks a-gape, the rows of shields along her sides more gaps than shields, salt stain and sea-bleach on her torn sails.

Not a man did they see at the haven. Not a man came to greet them as they drew *Sun-Swan* up on the strand. Not a man did they see as they trod the track up to King Gorm's hall.

The gate was fast shut. Thorkill took up the guest-horn that hung by it; he blew a loud blast.

The door of the hall did not open. But out from the porch came a door-ward, spear in hand.

"This is Thorkill of Iceland," said Thorkill, "and the shipmen of his ship, *Sun-Swan*."

"Lord," said the door-ward, "sad am I to tell you that you may not enter, nor may any of your men."

"I bring King Gorm news," said Thorkill. "At what time is it his will to see me, since I may not see him now?"

"Lord," said the door-ward, "it is his will not to see you at all. But Prince Gotrik begs that you will go to the guests' sleeping-room with your men, and he will come to you."

The guests' sleeping-room stood apart from the hall. So Thorkill and his shipmen went to it.

Soon came Prince Gotrik, and with his men with meat and drink.

"I am told the king has no wish to see me." said Thorkill. "Tell me, what can this mean?"

"That the Fima-Feng fear you," said Prince Gotrik. "But stay still for a time. For such is my father's love both of you and of marvels that I think the wind-vane will swing, in spite of them. Now tell me the news of your quest."

All that night the men sat up in the guests' sleeping-room. All that night the feast lasted. All that night Thorkill told the tale of his quests to Prince Gotrik. All that night Prince Gotrik sat, spellbound. And all that night at his feet, his eyes bright, sat Luf.

# How the Fima-Feng
# tried to slay Thorkill

As King Gorm sat at meat next day, Prince Gotrik said: "Never did I hear of such marvels as Thorkill has to tell of! It is sad, my father, that you, who so love marvels, may not hear them from his own lips!"

Then said King Gorm, with a sigh: "I was sad last night, my son, to turn such a hero from my door. Much do I long to see his face. Much do I long to hear his tale. I do not know now why I had such fear of him. I may yet send for him. I will sleep on it, and see."

At this, the five evil lords of the Fima-Feng fell into a fresh rage. When the meal came to an end, they drew apart to plot.

"Never shall we be free of Thorkill till he is dead," said Long-Man.

"That means he must die," said Lick-Pot.

"And *that* means we must slay him," said Ring-Man.

"But dare we, when Prince Gotrik leans so to him? asked Little-Man.

"If we can get the king to bid us slay him, we dare," said Thumb.

That night, the five lords again lit the king to his room. Torch in hand, they stood round the bed till they saw him fall into a doze too light to be true sleep.

Then Long-Man said, with one eye on King Gorm's still form: "See how our dear lord sleeps! For him we wish many more happy years of life. It is sad to think that the hour when he sees Thorkill will be his own death-hour."

"And that as long as Thorkill lives," said Lick-Pot, "our dear lord must live in fear."

"How is that so?" asked Ring-Man.

"As long as Thorkill lives," said Lick-Pot, "our dear lord lives in fear that one day he must see him. If he sees him, how can he help but hear his tale? If he hears his tale, how can he help but die?"

"Then he who slays Thorkill," said Little-Man, "will save our dear lord's life."

"Yet who will dare to slay Thorkill," asked Thumb, "unless our dear lord bids him do so?"

Then King Gorm said in a low hiss, his eyes still shut: "Slay him!"

"Our dear lord bids us slay him," said Long-Man.

"So slay him we will," said Lick-Pot.

"To save our dear lord's life," said Ring-Man.

"When shall we slay him?" asked Little-Man.

"This night, as he sleeps in his bed," said Thumb.

Then out of the king's room they crept.

Soon Prince Gotrik went in, to see how his father slept, as he did each night now the king grew so old and weak.

Then King Gorm came out of his light sleep; and all that the five lords had said wove in his mind like things out of a dream. And in his heart his love of Thorkill strove with his fear for his own life.

Tears fell from his dull old eyes as he felt this fight rage in him. As Prince Gotrik held his torch to look at the king, he saw the tears roll down his face.

"Why do you weep, my father?" Prince Gotrik asked.

"I had an ill dream, my son," the old king told him.

"What did you dream that was so ill?" asked Prince Gotrik.

"In my dream," the old king told him, "Thorkill was

to be slain as he slept in his bed this night. In my dream five men were to slay him. In my dream it was I who told them to slay him."

Then Prince Gotrik saw what must have come to pass.

He held the old king's hand till he slept again. Then he went to find Thorkill. He told him all King Gorm had told *him*.

"I read this as a plot of the Fima-Feng to slay you, and to lay the crime at my father's door," he said. "Yet I have no proof, so how can I accuse them of it? For all men know that my father's wits grow weak. So I beg of you, Thorkill, to fly and save your life."

"I will not fly, Prince," said Thorkill, "and yet I will save my life."

So that night, he lay in his bed till all the men in the sleeping-room slept. Then up he rose. In his place he put a log, and laid his bed-rug over it. Then he slid behind the bed.

All was still for a time. Then a faint creak came from the door; then a faint stir of the straw on the floor.

In the dark a dark shape bent to feel the dark shape that lay so still in the bed.

In the dark Thorkill saw a dull glint, as a battle-axe rose and fell.

Again a faint stir of the straw on the floor; again a faint creak from the door. Then all was still again.

Next day, King Gorm sat in his high-seat, old, weak, his wits astray. How much was dream? How much was not dream?

Now his love of Thorkill was more than his fear for his life. And now his fear for his life was more than his love of Thorkill.

Then into the hall came the five evil lords of the Fima-Feng. Such a sin-sly smile was on each face that all eyes were on them as they went up the hall. So only Prince Gotrik, at his father's side, saw Luf slip in behind the back of the door-ward.

The five lords came and stood in a bunch at the high-seat.

"King Gorm, all is well!" cried Long-Man.

"Let your fears be at rest!" cried Lick-Pot.

"For never now will Thorkill bring your death-hour with his dread news!" cried Ring-Man.

"You are rid of him now, Lord, as your will was!" cried Little-Man.

"For Thorkill was slain in the night!" cried Thumb.

"Was that my will?" cried the weak old king, aghast. "If it was, it was not I who spoke it, but the evil that is in me. Ah, Thorkill! Did you but live, what joy to see you stride into this hall!"

Then Prince Gotrik bent to set his arm round the weak old king, as he shook and wept on the high-seat. And as he held him up, he said: "That joy shall be yours, my father!"

At Prince Gotrik's nod, Luf slid to the door, and threw it wide. And in strode Thorkill, long and lean, as he strode in that first night, now so long ago.

"Thorkill! It is Thorkill!" the news ran down the hall.

The Fima-Feng swung round to look, wild and white of face.

"Lord," they cried out loud, "bear well in mind that Thorkill brings you your death-hour!"

But at the sight of Thorkill, the old king's face was bright with joy.

"What is to be, will be," he said. "If Thorkill bring me my death-hour, so let it be. I care not, if he comes!"

All eyes were now on Thorkill. The five evil lords drew apart.

"So," said Long-Man with a shrug, "the hour of our power is past."

"If this is so," said Lick-Pot, "we shall pay for last night with our lives."

"If this be so," said Ring-Man, "we shall do well to flee as soon as we can, *if* we can."

"We can get no steeds from the stable by night," said Little-Man.

"*Sun-Swan* lies in the haven," said Thumb. "Let us get such of our men as we can, and as much of our gold as we can, and put out to sea in her."

And this they did.

The wind still blew North. North, North it blew the ship, out of the smooth home-seas into the storm-seas that had swept away Thorkill's stores.

But *Sun-Swan* now was no longer fit to face such storm-seas. With no prow, with no ox-hide deck-roof, with rent sails, with planks agape, with frame made weak by loss of wood, she sank in the first storm.

The five lords of the Fima-Feng sank with her. No man on her ever came again to land.

# How Thorkill came again
# to King Gorm

When Thorkill's name had flown from lip to lip, a deep hush fell on the hall.

In that deep hush, up to the high-seat strode Thorkill. The red gem was bright as a fire in the arm-ring on his arm.

At his heels came Luf, his eyes bright, his new spear in his hand.

At Luf's heels came Onni, his left eye venom-blind, and Omd, his right arm venom-dried.

Thorkill's face was stern as he stood before King Gorm.

"King Gorm," he said, "for your sake did I fare forth to Giant-land. For your sake did I face many perils. Was it well done to repay me with a blow of a battle-axe? From the snares of Gudmund the Frost-giant I slid free. Must I now meet snares set for me by a king?"

At this the old king wept again.

"Heap no more shame on me, Thorkill," he cried. "The shame I feel is more than my old heart can well bear. But sit down with me on the high-seat. And tell me your tale of marvels that I so long, yet so fear, to hear."

Then Prince Gotrik gave up his seat to Thorkill, as on that night when he first came as night-guest. And Thorkill sat down at King Gorm's side.

And he told King Gorm all that had come to pass since *Sun-Swan* had set sail from his haven. He told of the storm in the storm-seas, and of how *Sun-Swan* had lost her stores so that the shipmen had been short of meat.

He told of how *Sun-Swan* swam to Herd-giant-land, and of how the shipmen held a strand-hew, and slew all the herd. He told how the giant herdsmen set a strand-hew fine that left them with no flint and steel in all the ship.

He told how the ship-fire went out as *Sun-Swan* swam on in the grey gloom, and how they saw the red star over Fire-giant-land. He told how he went to seek fire, and how the three black giants with the horny noses sold him a live brand and wise counsel for two home-truths.

He put out his arm, with Prince Gotrik's arm-ring on it; and he told how the red glow of its gem at the mast-head had led him back to the ship.

He told how they had no fat to bait the horns they were to throw to the giant dogs of Treasure-Town. He told how Luf sang to the seals, and how each seal gave up his life as a free gift, to give them seal-meat and seal-fat.

He told how they came to Frost-giant-land. He told how Gudmund the Frost-Giant met them with his giant sledge, and gave them much help, and yet laid traps to catch them.

He told of the ship-man who ate of Gudmund's food, and so was lost to them.

He told of the ship-man who drank of Gudmund's wine, and so was lost to them.

He told of the ship-man who took the hand of a giant maid in his, and so was lost to them.

He told how they went to Garfred's Treasure-Town, on its grey cliff. He told of the marvels they saw in Garfred's Treasure-Hall.

He told of Garfred's three chief treasures — the snake arm-ring, and the stag's horn of gems, and the mammoth tusk that cast up wine.

He told how three of the shipmen laid hands on them, and how the giants woke. He told of the fight with the giants in the Treasure-Hall, and of how only one in four of all his shipmen came out.

The old king sat spellbound as Thorkill told his tale. On the long wall-bench, all the king's men sat as spellbound.

Then Thorkill told of how Gudmund took them back to *Sun-Swan,* and how she swam on, out of grey gloom into black gloom, and so came at last to the Land of Utgard.

And at this, King Gorm the Old bent to Thorkill, and his dim old eyes grew bright as he cried:

"Ah, Utgard-Loki! Now do we come to the core of this tale of marvels! Tell on, of Utgard-Loki!"

Then Thorkill told of the foul black cave, and of the bats that slept in its roof, and the snakes that slept in its chinks. He told of the vast giant who slept in a pit, with bonds of lead on hands and feet, and a crown of lead on his head.

He told of the rune on that crown, and that the rune read *Utgard-Loki.*

At this, the old king's hand grew tight on Thorkill's arm. But his eyes never left Thorkill's face.

Then Thorkill told how they had tried to wake Utgard-Loki. He told how Luf had tried to pluck a hair from the giant's chin to wake him, and how the bats awoke, and the snakes awoke, but still not Utgard-Loki.

He told how each man hid under his ox-hides so that all came forth alive from the cave, and all, save two, safe and sound.

Then Thorkill bade Omd stand forth, and let the king see his venom-dried arm, and tell the king how he got it. And this Omd did.

Then Thorkill bade Onni stand forth, and let the king see his venom-blind eye, and tell the king how he got it. And this Onni did.

Then Thorkill bade Luf stand forth, and let the king see his spear, and tell him how he got it. And this Luf did.

Then from under his red fur cloak Thorkill took the rich cup that was King Gorm's gift to Utgard-Loki. He set it down on the table.

"Your gift to your god I bring you back, King Gorm," he said, "since I found no god to take it."

At this, King Gorm began to rock and to groan.

"Deep pain is it," he cried, "for a king to hear that the god he has put his trust in is but a foul giant that sleeps in bonds. And still I know not to what abode of the gods I can go when my death-hour is upon me!"

"My tale is not yet at an end, King Gorm," said Thorkill. "Till now I have told you of dark marvels. But I have still to tell you of marvels of the light."

Then Thorkill told how *Sun-Swan* lay ice-fast on the black strand till it came to Luf to bring to his mind the new God still to come.

He told of the kind wind that sprang up, and how it blew the ship back, out of black gloom into grey gloom, out of grey gloom into the first white light of the moon-way, and so at last into the bright day-light of the sun-blest life of men.

At this, the old king's sad face grew bright again with joy. He took up his gift-cup from the table, and bent his head over it, his eyes shut.

"From Utgard-Loki I take back this cup," he said. "I

give it to this God who is to come and who has such care for man."

Then Thorkill told how the kind wind blew *Sun-Swan* south past Denmark, to a safe landfall in Frankland, in the haven of Luf's father. He told how Luf's father had told them of the Shaven Man at Thor's Oak, and of how they rode out to hear his news.

He told of the Shaven Man who sat on the steps of the cross and sang the old lays of Iceland to his harp. He told of the Shaven Man's good news that the God who was to come *was* come. He told of Gem-Lea, the new God's hall made all of gems, a bright abode of joy that all men now might go to when they died.

At this a sigh of joy broke from the old king. But still he sat, his eyes shut, his head bent over the cup, a look of joy on his face.

Thorkill's tale came to an end. But still the king sat on, as if he slept.

At last, Prince Gotrik put out a hand to his father's. Only then did he find that the old king's death-hour had come.

"So the Fima-Feng spoke truth, Thorkill," said Prince Gotrik. "My father's death-hour *was* bound up with your news of marvels. Yet not with dread did his life go from him, but on a tide of joy. Glad was he of the abode he was to go to. Glad was he to go to Gem-Lea."

So King Gorm the Old died gently and with joy at the end of Thorkill's tale. And the good Prince Gotrik came to the throne of Denmark in his father's place.

When Thorkill came to bid him farewell, he said: "Stay with me, Thorkill. Much need has this land of men as brave and bold and good and lucky as Thorkill of Iceland."

"I will come back to you with joy, King Gotrik, if that

is your will," said Thorkill. "But first I must go to Frank-land. First I must hear all that the Shaven Man can tell me of the new God who now is come."

"Go, then," said King Gotrik. "And bring the Shaven Man back with you, if he will come. Tell him the Danes as well as the Franks have need of his good news."

"All men have need of it," said the Shaven Man, when Thorkill came to him and told him.

And with joy and good-will he went back to Denmark with Thorkill, and told his good news of the new God to King Gotrik and his men.

Then said King Gotrik: "Dip me in the river, Shaven One, for this new God shall be my god."

"Dip me, too," said Luf. "And if I may have two godfathers, I will have King Gotrik for one, and Lord Thorkill for the other. "

So into the river with King Gotrik the Good went Thorkill and Luf, and Onni and Omd, and Sild and Aldi, and Gok and Bok, and all the rest of Thorkill's shipmen, and many of King Gotrik's men.

And King Gotrik sent the Shaven Man all up and down the land, to bring his good news to the Danes.

With him went Luf, and sang of how Thorkill had help from the new God when he was ice-fast in Giant-land. And at the same time he sang with such love of the seals' gift to the shipmen that men gave him a new by-name, Luf Orkn, for in the speech of the North Lands, *orkn* means a big seal.

In this way did Thorkill's visit to Giant-land free the Danes from the grip of Utgard-Loki.

In this way did Thorkill bring to an end the Dusk of the Gods in Denmark.

In this way did he bring to Denmark the good news of the new God.

# The Dream of King Alfdan

*An Old Norse Hero-Tale*

# How Haki was made a Wolf's Head

King Sigurd the Hart was king of Ring-Rik in Norway.

At the birth of his son he held a splendid feast.

At the feast, King Sigurd sat in his high seat, and the newborn prince was laid at his feet. And King Sigurd gave the boy the name of Guthorm.

To this birth-feast came the two kings of the two lands next to Ring-Rik. They sat next to King Sigurd, at the top of the long table that ran the length of the long hall.

Next to the kings sat lords, in red furs and gold arm-rings. And next to the lords sat the men, in coats of mail.

The lords drank deep of wine from golden wine cups.

The men drank deep of ale, from ale horns bound with silver.

And the king's hall rang with songs and jests and mirth. Soon men who had drunk too deep began to sprawl and to brawl. They began to shout and to brag, and to pluck at dagger and sword hilt.

Ragnild, the new prince's sister, came in, to bring the king's wine in a guest-cup. She was only six years old. But even then she had the by-name of Ragnild the Golden, so gay a gold was her hair.

She gave the guest-cup first to the king next to her father. This was the young King Alfdan the Black. As he drank from it, she threw back her head to gaze at his black hair.

"Never did I see black hair till now," she said. "In Ring-Rik our hair is golden."

"Ah," said King Alfdan the Black, "but I have a golden roof, the only one in all Norway. My hall is by a lake; and in the sun you can see its roof flash like gold fire over the water."

"My father's grave mound will be by a lake," said the small princess. "A wise man told him that it must be by a lake, that it might help me in my hour of need."

King Alfdan gave her back the guest-cup. She gave it to the next king, King Eric the Merry. King Eric had red hair. His eyes were full of fun.

"What roofs do kings with red hair have?" asked the small princess.

"Roofs of straw, that birds can nest in," King Eric told her. "And the birds sing, to tell the kings with red hair things that will come to pass."

King Eric spoke in jest. Yet what he said was true. For he had the sight that can see a man's fate. And it was when the birds sang in his hall thatch that his gift came upon him.

"What do the birds sing about King Alfdan?" asked the small princess.

"They sing," said King Eric, "that he will dream a dream in a pigsty. The dream will only be a dream about his own hair. Yet with that dream will be bound up a new fate for all Norway."

"What do the birds sing about me?" asked the small princess.

"They sing," said King Eric, "that you will help to make that dream in the pigsty come true."

"What do the birds sing about you?" asked the small princess.

"They sing," said Eric, "that I, and this newborn Prince Guthorm, and that small boy who peeps in at the door, will all help to make the dream in the pigsty come true."

The small princess swept round to look at the boy at the door.

"That is Koll," she said. "He is my playmate. The lord next to you is his father. And the lord next to him is the father of those two big boys with Koll. They are Arek and Askel; they are my playmates, too. Will they help the dream in the pigsty to come true?"

"The birds did not say so," said King Eric, "so I do not think they will."

Koll's father shook the arm of the father of Arek and Askel. On his face was the flush of too much wine.

"Hear you that, Haki?" he cried. "My son will play a part in Norway's fate. But your sons will not."

"Say you so?" cried Haki, red with rage.

And in a flash his sword was out and had struck Koll's father a deathblow.

A hush fell then on all the hall. All eyes were on King Sigurd.

With a deep sigh, King Sigurd rose from his high seat.

"Haki," he said, "in one flash of rage you rob me of two good lords. For you know the law. For that thrust I must make you a wolf's head."

The small Princess Ragnild asked low of King Eric: "What is a wolf's head?"

King Eric bent and spoke into her ear: "An outlaw. He must give up his hall and his lands and all that is his. He has three days of grace; then all who see him will be free to slay him."

"Poor Haki!" said Ragnild the Golden. "Then what can he do?"

"All he can do," said King Eric, "is to flee from the

parts of the land that men dwell in. He must find a place to dwell in some wild part where men do not go."

And this was what Haki the Wolf's Head did.

When Haki fled, the small Princess Ragnild lost two of her playmates. For with Haki went his wife, and his men, and his two young sons.

To a wild part of Ring-Rik they rode, a part too wild for most men to dwell in. It was full of crags and cliffs; no green was to be seen.

In it they came to a wide cleft in the cliffs. From the foot of the steep cliffs, far, far below, came the rush and roar of swift water.

"On the far side of such a cleft," said Haki the Wolf's Head, "even a wolf's head will be safe."

It was too wide a gap for a man to leap on foot. But it was not too wide for a good steed. So over the cleft, from cliff top to cliff top, one by one, sprang Haki's band on Haki's steeds.

Then on they rode, till they came to a thick fir wood. And on among the fir trees they rode, till they came to a vast lake deep in the wood.

"In this wood will we dwell," said Haki the Wolf's Head. "On this side the lake will guard us, and on that side the steep cleft."

"Father," said Arek, "let us set a trip cord on our side of the cleft. Then if a steed springs over, the cord will jolt it as it lands. And that will cast its rider over the cliff into the river far below."

"No man who has no need to will seek to cross such a cleft," said Haki. "All the same, my son, a trip cord we will set. And it shall be yours, Arek, to look after."

So a trip cord was set. And each day Arek went to see that it had not been sprung. Soon Haki the Wolf's Head had a new hall, hidden deep in the fir wood. It was not as fine a hall as his old one; but it had a bower for his wife, and the bower had an inner room for her two young sons.

When Arek and Askel grew older, they left this inner room and went to sleep in the sleeping-room of the men. Then Haki's wife took the inner room to dry her herbs. For this she had need of a stream of air; so the men made her a round hole high in the wall. The Norse name for such an air hole in the old days was a "wind's eye."

Haki's wife used the herbs to heal the sick, for she was the leech in that hall of outlaws. When one of Haki's men was sick or hurt, he came to her to heal him. She had much skill in such things, as a lord's wife had in those days.

Arek was much with his father; but Askel was much with his mother. She saw, as he grew, that Askel had a love of herbs. So she took care to teach her skill to him, that he might take her place as leech to the outlaws when her time came to die.

From time to time, Haki and his outlaws went over the cleft by night. To the rich parts of Ring-Rik they rode, to rob and to raid. So they soon had good store of gold and of gear. Yet with such craft and skill did they make their raids that no man was able to track them back to the hall in the fir wood.

# How King Sigurd came
# to the outlaws

So ten years went by. Haki's wife died. Arek and Askel
began to grow up. In all that time, no boat came over
the lake. In all that time, no steed sprang over the
cleft. In all that time, no man in all Ring-Rik found
Haki's hall in the wilds.

So ten years went by. Then, one day at the end of
the fall, King Sigurd rode out alone to hunt the stag.

Such joy did he take in this that from it he had got
his by-name of Sigurd the Hart.

He had not ridden far when a tall stag ran by. And
off he set to hunt it.

Swift was the speed of the stag. Swift was the speed
of King Sigurd's steed. Over hill and dale sped the stag.
Over hill and dale sped King Sigurd after it.

By dusk the stag had led him into a part of his land
he did not know. All about him were vast crags and
steep cliffs; no green was to be seen.

The stag came to a wide, deep cleft in the cliffs.
From the foot of the cliffs, far, far below, came the rush
and roar of swift water.

Over the cleft, from cliff top to cliff top, sprang the
stag.

Over the cleft, from cliff top to cliff top, sprang King
Sigurd on his steed.

Across the far cliff top a trip cord ran. The stag
sprang clear of it. But King Sigurd's steed sprang into
it. So sudden and sharp was the jolt that the king was
thrown.

His head hit the crag as he fell. Over that steep cleft he hung, his left foot still held in its stirrup.

Still lay the king. Still stood the steed. Still were crag and cliff in the dusk all about them.

Then, with slow steps, the steed began to drag the king away from the cleft. Its hoof took the trip cord with it.

On went the steed, till it came to a thick fir wood.

Into this wood it went.

By now it was dark. Soon the full moon came up. Still on in the moonlit dark went the steed, deep into the wood.

Deep in the wood, hidden among the thick fir trees, the steed came to a hall.

At the door of the hall the steed came to a halt.

The door of the hall was shut. On it, with its hard front hoof, the steed gave three raps, loud and sharp.

Haki the Wolf's Head and his outlaws sat at meat in the hall. Pine brands lit along the walls cast a red glow on silver dish and golden wine cup, the spoil of the outlaws' raids.

At the sound of those three raps, the men sat stiff and still, ale horn in hand. The gaze of all went to the door.

"Our first guest in all our ten years here!" cried Haki. "Ten men to the door, and let us see this night guest!" The ten men next to the door rose from the table. They went to the door and slid back the bar that held it fast. All ten stood sword in hand as the door swung gently open.

From moonlit night to torchlit hall, with slow steps, King Sigurd's steed came in. By the left foot still held in the stirrup, it drew the prone king after it.

Up sprang the men from the table. But Haki cried

down the hall: "Each man stay in his place! Let Askel first tend this man!" Askel knelt by the king. He felt the king's head, his wrist, his brow. He laid his ear to the king's chest and to the king's lips.

Then he stood up.

"Father," he said, "this man is not yet dead. But so sore are his hurts that in three days he will be. It seems that he fell from his steed and broke his skull in the fall."

"That must have been at the cleft," said Arek, "for I see my trip cord on the steed's hoof."

"But why came he to the cleft?" asked Haki. "I do not think it was to seek us out, for it is long since our last raid."

"It may be that a stag led him," said Askel, "for he is clad for the hunt. And yet he can be no simple hunter. He has the look of a man of good birth."

At this, Haki rose and came down the hall. He bent low over the king. In the dim red glow, it was hard to see him plain.

"Bring me a torch!" cried Haki. Arek ran to him with a lit pine brand. He held it to the king's face.

"A man of good birth he is," said Haki. "I know this face well, even after ten years. For I was his man till he made me a wolf's head. This is King Sigurd the Hart!"

From lip to lip flew the name. All down the long bench a hubbub broke out: "If he is so near his death hour, who will rule Ring-Rik next? For Prince Guthorm is but ten years old."

"Ragnild the Golden is sixteen. She is of age to rule."

"But king's men look to be led by a king."

"Well, is she not of age to wed? The man who weds her will be king."

"Some man will have luck, then."

"Why not our Lord Haki?" At that, one and all took up the cry: "Let Lord Haki wed Ragnild the Golden! And let us all be king's men!"

Haki the Wolf's Head held up his hand. A hush fell.

"First things first," said Haki. "Askel, take four men and bear the king to a bed. Tend his hurts, and stay at his side."

Four men rose from the bench and came to King Sigurd. They took him up and bore him from the hall.

Askel the Leech went with them.

Then, with bent head, Haki trod the length of his hall, to and fro, to and fro. To and fro, to and fro, the eyes of his men went with him. In that long hall, the only sound was the tramp of Haki's feet.

Then he stood still. He threw up his head.

"This plan you din in my ears is a bold plan, men!" he cried. "We shall need to think it out well. But we will try it!" Back on his high seat, chin in hand, Haki made his plans, with Arek at his side to help him.

"The king's men will have no fear for the king as yet," said Haki. "For I call to mind that it has ever been his way, if the hunt took him far, to spend the night in the open."

"And I call to mind," said Arek, "that when he did this, it was ever Ragnild's way to ride out alone next dawn to meet him."

"Then she plays into our hands," cried Haki. "For we can whisk her away as she rides out at dawn and be back for the bride feast by sunset."

"We must take Prince Guthorm, too," said Arek, "lest, with the princess lost, the king's men make him king."

"When King Sigurd dies," said Haki, "the king's men

will not know it. The first they will know of it will be when Queen Ragnild rides into her hall, with King Haki at her side. So we do not need to take Prince Guthorm, if he is not with her. If he is with her, it will be best to take him too.

"Will you bring her by force, or coax her, or hoax her?" asked Arek.

"We will give her the true news that the king lies nigh to death," said Haki. "I think that then she will come of her own free will. Now Askel shall stay to tend the king, and a third of the men to deck the hall for the bride feast. Bid the rest bring out the steeds. We must be on our way in an hour if we are to meet my bride at dawn!"

# How the outlaws took
# Ragnild the Golden

At dawn the next day, Ragnild the Golden rode out from the king's hall to meet her father. She had grown tall and fair of face, and her hair was still as gay a gold as when she was a child.

"I will ride with you, sister," said the small Prince Guthorm. "For you need a man to guard you, now you are of age to wed."

Koll, Princess Ragnild's old playmate, was now King Sigurd's page.

"A ten-year-old shrimp of a lad is no guard for a golden princess," said Koll. "I think I had better come too, and guard you both."

So off all three set in the dawn.

Out they rode among the fields that had been full of ripe red corn a few weeks ago. On they rode, across the green vale that fed the cows. And so they came into a bright wood of silver birch trees.

As they rode in the wood, Ragnild the Golden held back her steed.

"Do you hear hoofbeats?" she asked.

Thud, thud, thud, came the beat of hoofs from far away.

"I know that hoofbeat," said the small Prince Guthorm. "It is our father's steed. How fast he rides home today!" Thud, thud, thud, came the hoofbeats, loud and louder, near and nearer. Then into sight, among the silver birch trees, came a steed.

"Yes," said Ragnild the Golden, "that is our father's steed. But is that our father on it?"

"It is not," said Koll. "It is someone I have never seen. And yet it seems to me that it is someone I did see, long ago."

As the rider came near to them, he drew his steed up sharp.

"Princess Ragnild!" he cried. "I come to you from King Sigurd the Hart. You will know this steed for his. And he sends you his ring."

He held out a ring to her.

"What ails my father?" cried Ragnild. "Yes, yes, this is his steed, and this his ring."

"He fell from his steed and is sore hurt," said the rider. "He lies now at my hall. I come to take you to him."

"Koll," said the princess, "ride back and fetch men to bear my father home. My brother and I will ride on with you, my lord. How is it that I do not know your face or name?"

Koll bent his brows as he swung around his steed to ride back to the hall. He felt he knew that man. And he felt he did not trust him.

And then it came to him who it was. He knew that face from when he was a child, ten years ago. He knew it for the face of the man who had slain his father.

"It is Haki the Wolf's Head!" he cried.

And he flung his dagger at Haki. It cleft Haki's mail. It went deep into his side.

Then from among the birch trees came steed after steed, each with its rider clad in mail, spear in hand and sword at side. Amid that sudden throng of men, the prince and princess did not see the spear flung after Koll. They did not see Koll fall.

118

One rider cried, as he rode to Haki's side: "Father, are you hurt?"

"I can last till Askel can tend me, Arek," said Haki.

"Arek!" cried Ragnild the Golden. "If this is true that your father tells me of my father, why is it with spears that you come to fetch me to him?"

"What my father tells you is true, Princess Ragnild," said Arek. "It is only with spears that we can come; for call to mind that we are outlaws. All men are free to slay us at sight, as you saw Koll seek to slay my father. Each of us risks his life, Princess, to bring you to the king."

Ragnild the Golden bit her lip and bent her head, for she saw that this was true.

"You are right," she said. "And much do I owe you all. Now let us ride to my father."

At a swift pace the throng of men set off, with the prince and princess in the midst of them. By secret by-ways they cut across the land to the wild, bare tract of crags and cliffs. They did not stop till they came to the wide, deep cleft, with its rush and roar of swift water far below.

"It was at this cleft that the king your father fell, Princess," said Arek. "Shall I bind you to your steed for the leap across?"

"No," said Ragnild the Golden. "I can sit my steed."

"Shall I bind you to your steed, Prince?" asked Arek.

"No," said the small Prince Guthorm. "I can sit my steed."

"Bind me, my son," said Haki, with a gasp. "For I am weak from loss of blood."

Arek bound his father to King Sigurd's steed. Over the wide cleft, from cliff top to cliff top, one by one, sprang the steeds.

"Do not unbind me, Arek, lest I fall," said Haki, his hand to his side. "Set up the trip cord when the last steed is over."

This Arek did. Then on and into the fir wood they rode. And so they came to Haki's hidden hall.

Cries and shouts of joy met them at the door of the hall. But the joy was cut short when the men who ran out saw Haki droop on his steed.

So weak was he now that his men had to lift him down and bear him into the hall.

"Bear me to my bed, men," said Haki. "Arek, bring our guests to the king. And send Askel to me. Tell him I have need of his skill."

Prince Guthorm's eyes were wide as he was led into the hall. For its long table was set with gold and silver, as if for a feast, and a blaze of cloth-of-gold lay on the long bench and on the high seat.

Across fresh straw Arek led the prince and princess to his mother's bower.

"It was my mother's way, when one of us was sick," he told them, "to tend him in her bower. So it is in her bower, that is now your bower, Princess, that we have laid the king."

As they came into the bower, Askel the Leech rose from his seat by the king's bed. Ragnild the Golden ran to meet him.

"Askel, how is my father?" she cried.

Askel bent low over her hands.

"Princess, he sleeps. He can last but a short time now," he said.

Ragnild laid her hand on her father's brow, then sank into Askel's seat. Here she sat, as still as the still form on the bed, till Arek came in with a silver bowl of water.

120

He knelt to wash the hands and feet of his guests, as was the way in the old days.

"That chest holds all my mother's gear, Princess," he said. "Take from it what you need. This inner room is yours, Prince. It was mine and Askel's when we were boys, and the chest in it is full of our gear from when we too were ten years old. Take what you need."

"My father's end is not far off," said Ragnild the Golden. "So set no place for me in the hall, Arek; I will stay with him till the end."

"You shall do as you will, Princess," said Arek.

And to himself he said, "Since the bride feast must be put off."

For as soon as Askel had seen the gash in Haki's side, he had told him: "Father, with this gash in your side you will hold no bride feast this night, nor for many nights to come."

"No matter, so I hold it in the end," said Haki. "Koll has put off the bride feast. But I still hold Ring-Rik's new queen."

# How Princess Ragnild
## saw the golden roof

That night, as the princess sat at his side, King Sigurd the Hart died in his sleep. Ragnild the Golden wept over him. Then she took the king's ring and set it on the small Prince Guthorm's thumb.

"For you are king of Ring-Rik now, little brother," she told him.

But Prince Guthorm drew the big ring from his thumb and gave it back to her.

"Wear it for me, Ragnild," he said. "I am too small yet to be a king. Koll calls me just a ten-year-old shrimp of a lad, and Koll is right."

"What ails Koll, that he takes so long to bring our father's men?" asked Ragnild. "We have need of them now to seek a lake, and to make our father's grave mound at its side."

But when she said this to Arek, he told her: "Princess, a lake lies but a stone's cast from this hall.

Our men will make the king's grave mound at its side for you.

"Take me to this lake," said Ragnild the Golden, "that I may find the right place for my father's bones to lie."

"Then come with me now," said Arek. "At this dawn hour our men go to the lake to draw water."

So out into the dawn went the princess and the small prince, with Arek and the men with the water butts. Two and two they went along the track among the fir trees, the track that led away from the cleft.

Soon they came to the end of the track. To the left stood the wild, thick wood. To the right stood the wild, thick wood. And in front lay a lake so vast that it was water, water, water, all the way to the far sky.

Along the bank the men spread out, to fill the water butts. To and fro at the lakeside went Ragnild the Golden with slow steps and bent head, till she knew she had found the place for her father's grave mound.

"Let it be here," said she.

So in Ragnild's bower, King Sigurd the Hart lay in state. And at the lakeside, Haki's men cut down fir trees and made a round room in the ground for King Sigurd the Hart to sit in, with gold and gear, and with sword and shield, and with all that a king in the old days took with him into his grave.

And still Koll and the king's men did not come to the hall in the wilds. So it was Haki's men who set King Sigurd the Hart in the round room, and over it made a mound, wide and high, to mark the grave of a king.

Then said Ragnild the Golden to Arek: "Now that my father is laid to rest, I must go back to his hall with my brother, that he may be made king. And his first act as king shall be to give back to Lord Haki his lands, and to give all in this hall free pardon."

But Arek said: "Princess, it is not my father's will that your brother be made king. He wills that you be queen. And he wills that you stay here till he is well. And then he wills to wed you.

"Haki wills to wed me?" cried Ragnild the Golden. "Has Koll's dagger sent him mad?" She swung round in rage, and swept into her bower, and shut the door with a bang.

Out from the inner room came the small Prince Guthorm. He came with a slip and a slide, for he had boy's skates on his feet.

"Look, Ragnild!" he cried. "I found skates that fit me in Arek's chest. They must have been his when he was my age. Why, Ragnild! Why are you in such a rage?" Then Ragnild sank into a seat and drew him to her, and told him all that Arek had said.

As he sat and took off the skates, Guthorm said: "I think this plot must have been in Haki's mind from the first; for as we came into the hall, I saw that it was laid for a feast. I think it would have been your bride feast, Ragnild, had not Koll's dagger put it off."

"How can Haki dream he can make me wed him," cried Ragnild, "when he knows Koll is on his way to us with a band of our father's men?"

"But is Koll on the way?" asked Prince Guthorm. "If this plot was in Haki's mind from the first, then he left no men in the birch wood, to guide our men to this hall. If this plot was then in Haki's mind, it may be that he had Koll slain, so that now our own men have no clue as to what befell us."

"If what King Eric said at your birth feast was true," said Ragnild, "Koll cannot be slain. For Koll was to help to make the dream in the pigsty come true."

"It is Koll who has put off the bride feast," said Guthorm. "It may be that that was his help. Our men must have ridden far and wide by now to seek us, Ragnild, but I think this hall is too well hidden for them ever to find it. Shall we not try to slip out and find our own way back?"

"The door of my bower is our only way out," said Ragnild. "Go, Guthorm, and try that door. I fear you will find that a bar has been set across it."

The small prince set down the skates and ran to try the door. A bar on the far side held it fast.

"You are right, Ragnild," he said. "This way we cannot go. But my room has a wind's eye. If we can get up to it, we can slip out by that."

"We can, if you have a spell to make me as small as you, little brother," said Ragnild with a sad smile. "For I am far too big as I am to slip out of a wind's eye."

"Then I will go," said Guthorm, "and bring our men back to free you."

"And will you fly across the cleft to fetch them?" asked Ragnild, with her sad smile.

"No, I will steal a steed from the stable," said the small prince.

"First you must put the stablemen to sleep," said Ragnild.

Then said the small Prince Guthorm: "Since we can find no way to cross that cleft, we must try the other way."

"And how will you cross the lake?" asked Ragnild. "I saw no boat by the bank. Will you grow wings?"

A flick of Prince Guthorm's hand swept aside the skates, and they fell with a clang.

"Why, Ragnild!" he cried. "It is the end of the fall. In a week or two we shall see ice on the lake. Then I shall not need boat or wings; I can cross on Arek's skates!" Ragnild the Golden bent and gave him a hug.

"Ah, if we did but know what is on the far side!" she said with a sigh. "It may well be a wild land, as this is, too wild for good men to dwell in."

Prince Guthorm sat at her feet, his small chin in his small hand. He was still for a time.

"Ragnild," he said at last, "tell me again what the wise man told our father about his grave mound."

"He told him," said Ragnild, "that it must be at the side of a lake, that it might help me in my hour of need."

"Then seek its help," said the small prince. "For it seems to me that this is your hour of need."

When it was time to eat, the door of the bower swung open and men came in with rich food in a golden dish and with wine in golden wine cups.

As Princess Ragnild took the food, she said to them: "Tell Lord Arek it is my wish, when next you go to draw water, to go with you to my father's grave to pray."

"We will tell him, Princess," said the men.

So again the prince and the princess went out into the wood with Arek and the men with the water butts. Two and two they went along the track among the fir trees. But with them this time, in front and at the back, went men with spears.

When they came to the lake, the men spread along the bank to draw water.

"I will go to the top of the mound alone," said Prince Ragnild. "My brother will stay here with you, below."

The men with the spears spread to stand round the foot of the mound. With slow steps and bent head, Ragnild the Golden went up its slope. She came to the crest, and sat down to look about her. It was as if she sat on the top of a small hill.

She let her mind grow still, that if any help came, she might hear it. As she sat, looking on the water, the sun came out. And far away in front of her, she saw a flash of gold.

"What can that be?" she asked herself. "It came like a flash of gold fire over the water."

And then her mind went back ten years. She saw her

father's hall at the newborn Guthorm's birth feast. She saw herself, a small princess six years old, come in with the golden guest-cup. She saw herself give the guest-cup to a king with black hair.

"Never did I see black hair till now," said that small princess. "In Ring-Rik our hair is golden."

And what was it that the king with the black hair had said back to her? Her eyes grew bright as it all came back: "Ah, but I have a golden roof, the only one in all Norway. My hall is by a lake; and in the sun you can see its roof flash like gold fire over the water."

So now she knew that King Alfdan of Hadland had his hall on the far side of the lake. It came to her then that the outlaws did not know this. It came to her that what she had seen was a secret. She saw that to see that flash you had to be high in the air, as she was on the crest of her father's grave mound. Down below, on the bank, that gold fire did not show.

When Ragnild and Guthorm were in her bower again, Guthorm asked: "Did our father's grave mound help in your hour of need, Ragnild?"

"It did, little brother," she told him. "I know now that all will yet be well with us. For on the far side of the lake dwells the king who is to dream the dream in the pigsty."

# How Prince Guthorm went for help

Each night after that, when the prince and the princess were left alone and the bar held the bower door fast, they swept the straw from part of the floor. Then, in the dust, Ragnild the Golden drew a map of the sky, to teach the small prince how to find his way across the lake with the help of the stars.

Each day the prince and the princess went to the lake with the men who went to draw water. When Ragnild had sent to say that this was her wish, Askel the Leech had said to Haki: "It is good to let them do this, Father. For at the king's hall the princess was much out-of-doors; if she lacks fresh air now, she may well fall sick. With Arek and the men about them, they cannot slip away."

Day by day the cold grew, till the day came when they went out to find snow in deep drifts on the track. And soon after this came the day when they stood on the bank of the lake and saw in front of them one vast sheet of ice.

That day Arek said, as they went back: "In three days, Askel tells me, our father can rise from his bed and hold his bride feast. In three days, Princess, you will be my stepmother, and you, Prince, my small uncle!"

As soon as they were alone for the night, Ragnild the Golden said: "It must be soon now, Guthorm, or we shall be too late."

"Let it be now," said the small prince. "It is full moon, and that will be all to the good."

He took Arek's skates from the chest, and set thick

furs about him. Ragnild gave him a kiss. She gave him a hug.

They set a bench by the wall of the inner room, so that it stood under the wind's eye. They stood on the bench; into her arms Ragnild took him, to lift him to the wind's eye.

As she held him up, he was just able to stretch and reach to the high round hole. He was just able to cling and to hang from it by his hands.

"May Ull, the god of snowshoes, be with you, little brother," said Ragnild the Golden.

Prince Guthorm drew his small form up to the wind's eye. He got out one foot to the far side. He got out both feet to the far side. Out he went. Over he went. He hung and clung by his hands in the sharp night air.

Moss grew on the outer wall of the hall. Grass grew on the outer wall of the hall. So it was not hard for Guthorm to find footholds. It was not hard for him to find handholds.

Inch by inch down the wall slid the small prince, till his foot felt the soft snow on the ground.

Into the moonlit fir wood he stole. The footprints left by the men that day were black in the white snow. Along the track they led him, among the fir trees, to the lake.

He stood on the bank of the lake, at the foot of his father's grave mound, and he drew in a deep, deep breath.

To the left he saw a long, long plain of ice stretch away, away, away, to melt into the far dark.

To the right he saw a long, long plain of ice stretch away, away, away, to melt into the far dark.

In front he saw a long, long plain of ice stretch away, away, away, to melt into the far dark.

He bent, and bound his skates to his feet.

Up he stood, and drew his furs about him. Then, as light as a bird, and as swift as a bird, he began to skim across that moonlit, misty, vast white plain of ice.

So fast he flew that his swift flight made a wind.

Chill, chill, chill, blew that wind. Even with Arek's furs about him, Guthorm felt that chill creep into his bones. So fast he flew, and so vast was the plain he flew over, that it began to seem as if it was in a dream that he flew. The white light of the moon, the white mist, the white ice, all were like something in a dream.

So clear were the stars that he was able to match them with the map of the sky he had laid up in his mind, night by night. He was able to steer his track by them.

So bright a light did the full moon give that after a time he was able to make out dim forms along the sky line, far in front of him. On he flew; he saw now that the dim, dark forms were trees.

Still on he flew. The trees drew near; the trees grew clear.

At last, in the long dark line of trees, he saw a gap. And in the gap he saw the light of the moon gleam on a roof, part white with snow, part bright with gold, that was set among the trees.

And such was his joy that he sang out loud: "I have come across the lake from Ring-Rik to Hadland! I have found the hall with the golden roof of King Alfdan the Black!"

He drew in to the bank. Stiff and sore, he came up off the ice on to the snow. He unbound his skates. Up the slope he went, and under the porch to the door of King Alfdan's hall.

He felt for the guest horn that hung at the side of the door. He set it to his lips. He blew a blast on it.

The door swung wide. In from the moonlit night, with slow, stiff steps, went a small lad clad in furs, a pair of skates in his hand.

A hush fell on the men about the fires as the lad went up the hall and stood in front of the high seat. On the high seat sat King Alfdan. So black was his hair that the lad threw back his head to gaze at it.

"Never did I see black hair till now," he said. "In Ring-Rik our hair is golden."

"A small princess said the same to me ten years ago," said King Alfdan.

"That was at my birth feast," said the small prince. "I am Prince Guthorm of Ring-Rik. My father, King Sigurd the Hart, is dead. Haki the Wolf's Head holds my sister. In three days he wills to wed her, that he may take the land for his own."

"You sway on your feet, Prince," said King Alfdan. "Sit, eat, and drink. Then tell me all your tale."

Stiff and sore, the small prince sat. He ate. He drank. He told the king all his tale. Then he went to sleep with his head in the dish.

Said Torlef, King Alfdan's wise man: "Let him sleep, lord. A grown man might well be worn out by what this lad has made his small self do this night."

King Alfdan cried down the hall: "Let each man bring out his sledge, to cross the lake to Ring-Rik."

The small prince still slept as Torlef took him up and bore him out to the king's sledge.

"Let him sleep, lord," he said again. "We have no need of him yet. The marks of his skates on the ice will guide us over the lake."

And in Torlef's arms the small prince still slept as

the sledge sped over the vast plain of ice, with three of King Alfdan's strong steeds to pull it, as swift as black birds in the moonlight.

Not till the sledge drew up by King Sigurd's grave mound on the far bank of the lake did Torlef the Wise wake the lad.

"We need your help now, Prince Guthorm," he told him. "Show us the way to Haki's hall."

They left a small band of men with the steeds. The rest the small prince led along the track among the fir trees.

All was still in Haki's hall. Deep sleep held the out laws as King Alfdan broke in.

Short and sharp was the fight. To left and to right the outlaws fell, as the small prince led Torlef the Wise to the door of the bower, and slid back the bar.

"Ragnild! Ragnild!" he cried.

Then he was with her. Her arms were about him.

Her gay gold hair was about him.

With Torlef he led her out into the free air of the moonlit night. He ran with her along the track to the lake.

He set her in the king's sledge.

Then King Alfdan came back to his sledge. Back to their sledges came King Alfdan's men.

Then up from his sickbed rose Haki the Wolf's Head. He took up his sword.

Out to the stable he crept. He found King Sigurd's steed. Down to the edge of the lake he rode, asway in his saddle, his sword asway in his hand.

They saw him loom, black in the moonlight. They saw the steed slip as it set a hoof on the ice. They saw Haki thrown from his saddle, as Sigurd the Hart had been thrown. They saw Haki fall on his sword at the foot of King Sigurd's grave mound.

He knew then that his death hour was upon him.

"You have won my princess from me, Alfdan the Black," he cried. "But when you reach the age that I am now, take heed. Take heed, lest ice bring you to your death then, as now it brings me to mine."

And with that he died.

"Lord," said Torlef the Wise to King Alfdan, "let us take this wolf's head with us, and give him a hero's grave. Thus you may get free from his death-wish."

So they took up Haki and set him in the sledge.

"How old was Haki, Guthorm?" asked King Alfdan.

"Forty years old," the small prince told him.

"Ah, then," cried King Alfdan, gay of mood, "I have twice seven years to live till I need fear this ice fate!" Then back across the lake they went to the hall with the golden roof.

# The Queen's dream and the King's dream

When he got back to Hadland, King Alfdan the Black gave Haki the Wolf's Head a hero's grave.

A round room was dug for him at the lakeside, south of the hall with the golden roof, by the Place of the Cattle Branding. A mound was made over it, to mark the grave of a hero.

The day after the flight across the ice, King Alfdan the Black got up at dawn to greet the sun.

When he went to go out by the sunrise door of his hall, he found the bar drawn back. And when he went out, a golden princess stood by the wall, to greet the sun with him.

Then King Alfdan first saw plain, after ten years, the princess he had sped over the ice to save. And Princess saw plain, after ten years, the king who had sped over the ice to save her. And each fell in love with the other.

So they were wedded.

As they sat at the bride feast, the small Prince Guthorm came up the long hall to them. He stood in front of the high seat as he had stood the first time he had come this hall with the golden roof: "I bring you a vow as a bride gift," he said.

"What vow is that, little brother?" asked the new Queen Ragnild.

Then said the small prince: "When I am a man, the land of Ring-Rik will be mine. But I vow never to be its king. I give it to you, Alfdan and Ragnild, to add to your own land of Hadland."

"That is a kingly bride gift," said King Alfdan. "And why give us all you have of your own?"

"For the sake of both lands," said the small prince "For it seems to me that when two small lands have each a king, both lands are weak. But when two small lands have the same king, both lands are strong."

Then said Torlef the Wise: "This lad is small, but he is as wise as he is brave. This deed of his may well be the seed of a new fate for all Norway."

So the small prince dwelt with King Alfdan and Queen Ragnild in the hall with the golden roof. So wise was he in his ways, and such skill did he show in swordcraft as he grew, that Torlef said to King Alfdan: "As soon as he is of age to lead men, you will do well, lord, to set him over all your own men."

"This will we do," said King Alfdan, "the day he is sixteen winters old."

So time went on, till Ragnild the Golden had been a queen for three years. Then, one night, she had a dream.

In her dream, she stood in her garden. And as she stood, she felt the prick of a thorn. She felt for the thorn, and drew it forth from her dress.

As she held the thorn in her hand, it began to grow. It grew at both ends. It grew up; it grew down.

So much did it grow, so fast did it grow, that soon it had grown into a vast tree.

One end of the thorn went down among the grass.

Deep, deep, deep, into the ground it went, till the tree had long, firm roots.

The other end of the thorn grew high in the air. The trunk grew thick. Far across the sky it spread long, strong twigs.

In her dream, Queen Ragnild saw that the roots of

this vast tree were as red as blood. She saw that the trunk was as green as grass. She saw that the twigs were as white as snow.

She saw that so vast was the tree that from her garden it spread out over all the long land of Norway.

At dawn, Queen Ragnild told this dream to King Alfdan. King Alfdan told it to Torlef the Wise. For Torlef the Wise had much skill in dreams.

"How read you this dream, Torlef?" asked the king.

"I read it thus, lord," said Torlef. "From the queen shall spring a king who shall hold sway over all Norway."

"That will be a high fate," said King Alfdan. "But why are the roots of the tree as red as blood?"

Then said Torlef the Wise: "Lord, I take the tree to be a son the queen will bear. And I take the blood-red roots to mean that in his first years, his root-years as king, blood will be shed to make those roots root strong and firm."

"And why a trunk as green as grass?" asked the king.

"I take the green trunk," said Torlef, "to mean that in this king's mid-years the land will be rich and bear good crops."

"And why is the top of the tree as white as snow?" asked King Alfdan.

"I take the snow-white top," said Torlef, "to mean that this king will live to be very old, with hair as white as snow."

"Why do I not dream such dreams?" asked King Alfdan.

"It may be," said Torlef, "that you do not sleep in the right place for dreams. Did not the birds in his hall thatch sing to King Eric the Merry of a dream in a pigsty? When I wish to dream, I go and sleep in my pigsty."

"Then so will I," said the king.

So that night King Alfdan went to sleep in the pigsty. He lay on clean straw by the pigs. He slept. And in his sleep he had a dream.

In his dream, King Alfdan saw himself. He saw new locks of hair spring out of his head. Some grew down to his heel. Some grew to his shin. Some grew to his knee. Some grew to his hip. Some grew to his chest. Some grew to his neck. Some were but wisps that sprang out from the crown of his head.

But one lock was so long that it grew right down to the ground.

Now King Alfdan's own hair was as black as night. But in his dream, only a few of his locks were black. Some were brown. Some were red. Most of them were golden. One lock was so fair that it stood out among the rest. It was as pale as flax.

This flax-pale lock was the same lock that grew right down to the ground.

Next day at dawn, King Alfdan left the pigsty and stood at the sunrise door of his hall to greet the sun. Then he went to find Torlef the Wise. He told him his dream.

"How read you this dream in the pigsty?" he asked.

"I read it thus," said Torlef, "that from you will spring a race of kings that shall rule the land with power."

"And the long locks and the short locks?" asked King Alfdan.

"As some of the locks were long and some short," said Torlef, "so some kings shall rule with more power and some with less."

"And the fair lock so long that it grew down to the ground?" asked King Alfdan.

"As that lock is longer than the rest," said Torlef, "so shall that king rule with more power than the rest. From the queen's dream we know that he will be the first king to bring all Norway under his sway, and that he will be your son."

"I long to meet this son! May he come soon!" And soon he came. In less than a year a son was born to King Alfdan and Queen Ragnild.

The boy was not black of hair, as his father was. Nor was he gold of hair, as his mother was. So fair was his hair that it was as pale as flax.

They gave him the name of Harald. And from his flax-pale hair he got, even as a child, the by-name of Harald Hair-Fair.

King Alfdan was thirty years old when his son was born. The boy grew into a strong child, big of frame, bold and brave, with skill in all sports. So all went well till the winter when he was ten years old and his father, King Alfdan, was forty.

When the days grew cold at the end of the fall that year, Torlef the Wise said to King Alfdan: "Lord, take heed of the ice this winter. We gave Haki the Wolf's Head a hero's grave. This winter will show if that freed you from his death-wish."

# Who stole the King's Yuletide feast?

At the beginning of that winter, King Alfdan sent a branding-iron to each farm and hall in Hadland. This was to bring the news that it was time to hold a cattle branding.

So, as soon as the ice had set on the lake, from all parts of the land men came to the Place of the Cattle Branding. And each man drove his cattle before him.

For the ten-year-old Prince Harald, this was a time of high glee. The plain of ice at the foot of Haki's grave mound was a mass of tossing backs, with wave on wave of tall white horns riding on its crest. The air was loud with new sounds — the blare of bulls, the shouts of the cowherds, the ring of hoofs on the ice.

The small prince ran in and out among the cattle. He threw ropes to help to hold them. He fed the fires with pine logs. He held branding irons in the flame to heat them. He sang songs round the fires with the cowherds.

Among the cowherds that year was a Finn. He was small and slight and dark. His name was Ross.

No other cowherd told such tales as Ross the Finn.

No other cowherd sang such songs as Ross the Finn.

Ross the Finn knew runes that were able to call up mists and snow and winds.

Ross the Finn knew runes that were able to hide the sun, and to make a bare tree seem to be in full leaf.

For in Norway in the old days it was held that all Finns were troll-wise. To be troll-wise was to have skill in witchcraft.

No other cowherd of them all was so good with cattle as Ross the Finn. He knew how to heal a cow of all her ills. With him bulls were as tame as lambs. So, when the cattle branding was over, King Alfdan kept him with him as one of his own cowherds.

And now Prince Harald spent all his time with Ross the Finn.

No more did he come to his uncle, Prince Guthorm, that he might teach him swordcraft. No more did he come to Torlef the Wise, that he might teach him book-lore. No more did he come to his father, King Alfdan, that he might teach him things of state.

But he came to Ross the Finn, that he might teach him runes, and songs, and how to skate, and how to ski.

Ross the Finn made Prince Harald snowshoes and skates of bone. They had a curl in front, like the prow of a ship. Ross the Finn spoke runes over them.

"Now they will bear you to what place you will, little prince," said Ross the Finn.

Yuletide came round. In King Alfdan's hall the long table was set for the yuletide feast. The air was full of rich steams and of rich smells. The fires were ablaze down the hall. The walls were hung with cloth-of-gold; the table was bright with the gleam of gems and of gold and of silver.

King Alfdan and Queen Ragnild sat on the high seat.

Next to them sat Prince Guthorm and Torlef the Wise. But the small Prince Harald sat at the foot of the table, at the side of Ross the Finn.

And then, as the men sat down, and took up meat daggers, and put out hands to full ale horns, all in the blink of an eye, the table was as bare as a bone. Meat and drink, dish and wine cup, gem and gold and silver, all went into thin air.

"Witchcraft!" cried King Alfdan.

And from lip to lip, all down the long table, flew the cry: "Witchcraft! Witchcraft!" The eyes of all went to the small, dark man at the foot of the table — to the cowherd, Ross the Finn.

Then King Alfdan sent a thrall down the hall to bid Ross the Finn come to him.

Ross the Finn rose, and went up the hall, and stood in front of the high seat. The small Prince Harald rose with him. He went up the hall with him. He stood in front of the high seat with him.

King Alfdan was in a black mood. His black brows drew down over his black eyes. It was clear to see that it was not only from his black hair that he had got his by-name of Alfdan the Black.

"What hand had you in this, Finn?" he cried.

"Lord, no hand at all," said Ross the Finn.

King Alfdan gave a shout of rage. "But you are troll-wise. In all this hall, Finn, only you are troll-wise. If you had no hand in it yourself, still only you can tell me who took the feast from my table."

"Lord, that is not mine to tell you," said Ross the Finn.

"That you shall tell me, Finn!" cried King Alfdan.

Ross the Finn stood still in front of the high seat. His eyes met the eyes of the king. He made no sound.

"Take him," said King Alfdan to his thralls. "Bind him hand and foot. Cast him into the cave room under the hall. No meat shall he have, no drink shall he have, till he tells me who took the feast from my table."

"No, Father! No, no, no!" cried the small Prince Harald.

And he tried to cling to Ross the Finn.

But King Alfdan set a strong hand on his son's arm as the thralls took Ross the Finn away.

They bound him hand and foot. They cast him into the cave room under the hall. They shut the cave room door. They slid the bar to bolt him in.

Then twice a day King Alfdan went to the door of the cave room and asked Ross the Finn: "Who took the feast from my table?" And twice a day Ross the Finn told him: "Lord, that is not mine to tell you."

On the third day, when King Alfdan had left the hall, the small Prince Harald crept to the door of the cave room, and put his mouth to its chink.

"Ross, it is I, Harald," he said in a low tone.

"Help me, little prince!" said Ross the Finn, with a gasp. "Beg the king to let me have meat and drink, or I shall die."

Prince Harald ran after King Alfdan. He cast his arms about his father's knees.

"Father, let Ross have meat and drink, I beg you," he cried. "If you do not, he will die."

"Meat and drink he shall have," said King Alfdan the Black, "when he tells me who took the feast from my table."

Then in his mind the small Prince Harald made a vow: "Meat and drink shall my Finn have from my own hands!"

That night Prince Harald got into his bed still clad. When all was still, he rose. He stood at the door of his room and held his breath and listened. Deep sleep lay on King Alfdan and on all his men.

Prince Harald crept out to the hall. The pine brands

along the walls had all burnt out, but a small red glow still came from the dead fires. By that small red glow he was able to see.

Food from last night's meal lay still on the long table. Drink from last night's meal still stood on the long table. Prince Harald set a meat dagger in his belt. Full dish and full ale horn he took in his two hands.

He crept to the door of the cave room. He put his mouth to its chink.

"Ross, it is I, Harald," he said in a low tone.

He set down the dish and the ale horn, and slid back the bar that held the door fast. Into the cave room he crept.

Ross the Finn lay in the dark, bound hand and foot. The small prince felt him all over till he found his bonds. Then he drew the meat dagger from his belt and cut him free from them.

Then back he crept to the door, for the dish and the ale horn.

Ross the Finn sat up and took them. In the dark he ate and drank, and was glad and full of thanks.

"If I let you out, Ross," said Prince Harald, "can you get safe away?"

"With skates I can," said Ross the Finn.

"Skates you shall have," said the small prince. "But have you a secret place you can hide in from my father? I do not think any place in all Hadland will be safe if he stays in his black mood."

"I need not stay in Hadland," said Ross the Finn. "I can go south over the lake to King Eric the Merry in Ordland."

"Ah, that good King Eric!" said Prince Harald with a sigh. "So good, so kind, so merry, no black moods. What luck to have such a father! I wish I, too, might meet him."

"Then why not come with me to him now?" said Ross the Finn. "For it will go hard with you if you are here when the king your father finds you have set me free."

"Can a ten-year-old boy skate so far?" asked the small prince.

"Did not a ten-year-old Prince Guthorm skate from Ring-Rik to Hadland?" said Ross the Finn. "Then cannot a ten-year-old Prince Harald skate from Hadland to Ordland?"

"I will come, Ross," said Prince Harald. "Wait, while I fetch us skates and furs."

When he came back with the furs and the skates, Prince Harald said: "Let us go out by the sunset door. That bar is less hard to lift."

They set the bar back in place on the door of the cave room. They crept to the west door of the hall. They slid back the bar inch by inch, so that it made no sound. Inch by inch, they drew the door open. Out into the fresh night air they crept. Inch by inch, they drew the door shut.

At the edge of the lake they bound their strong skates to their feet. Then Ross the Finn took Prince Harald's right hand in his own right hand. In his left hand he took his left.

Then, side by side, the small dark Finn and the small fair prince began to skate south by night to Ordland.

# How Prince Harald
# went to King Eric

Over the ice, under a black sky full of sharp silver stars, sped the small Prince Harald and Ross the Finn.

The boy put up his head to sniff the fresh night air.

"The air is mild for Yuletide," he said. "Will the ice hold, think you?"

"Oh yes; the wind is mild, but not so mild as to bring a thaw," said Ross the Finn. "All the same, we must take heed as we skirt the foot of Haki's grave mound."

"Why so?" asked the small Prince Harald.

"Haki's grave mound looks over the Place of the Cattle Branding," said Ross the Finn. "And it is in such a place that the thaw will set in first."

"Why so?" asked the small prince again.

"At the cattle branding, cattle dung fell on the ice," said Ross the Finn. "It eats its way into the ice; it makes it soft and weak. Ah, did you not feel the ice give then under your skate?"

"A little," said Prince Harald. "It was just here, then, that you and I first met, Ross, just under Haki's grave. Then the ice was full of men and cattle, and the air was full of the blare of bulls and the shouts of cowherds. Now only you and I are here, and the air is as still as the grave — as Haki's grave."

Ross the Finn gave a slight shiver.

"Why do you shiver?" asked the small prince. "You are not cold?"

"No," said Ross the Finn. "But you know that all

Finns are a little troll-wise; and troll-wise men can see some things that are to come to pass. And when you said the air was as still as the grave, I saw that this Place of the Cattle Branding was soon to be a grave."

"So long as it is not yours or mine," said Prince Harald. "If you are troll-wise, Ross, then you knew all the time who took the yule feast from my father's table?"

"I knew, but it was not mine to tell him," said Ross the Finn.

"Can you tell me?" the small prince asked.

"You I can tell; for when next you sit at table, you will eat of that feast," said Ross. "It was King Eric the Merry."

"But why did he take it?" asked Prince Harald. "Is he so poor that he had no yule feast of his own?"

"King Eric is not rich as your father is rich," said Ross the Finn. "His hall has no golden roof. Nor is he so poor that he has need of any other king's yule feast. He took your father's feast, my prince, to draw you to him by a kind of magic after it."

"Then it is his wish that I go to him?" cried Prince Harald. "Then why did you not tell me so? And why did he not send for me?"

"If he is to help you, my prince," said Ross the Finn, "the will to go to him had to be yours."

"To help me? In what way is King Eric to help me?" asked Prince Harald.

"You have a high fate," said Ross the Finn. "But it seems it is a fate you may well let slip your mind. And King Eric can only help you to reach out to it if you come to his hall when you are ten years old."

"But how did he know I might not reach out to it?" asked Prince Harald. "He has never seen me, or I him."

"The birds that nest in his hall thatch have sung to tell him so," said Ross the Finn.

"If King Eric has such gifts," said the small prince, "why is he not rich? It seems to me he has it in his power to bend both men and things to his own ends."

"It is not his will to be rich," said Ross the Finn. "And never will he turn his troll gifts to self-gain, but only to the good of others."

"Yet with all this," said Prince Harald, "men say no king is so merry."

"That is so," said Ross. "His is a merry hall. His red beard is awag with jests from dawn to dark."

"All his hall seems to have need of," said Prince Harald, "is a prince of my own age for me to play with."

"It has no small prince, but it has a small princess," Ross told him. "She is the same age as you; she has red hair, like her father; she is gay and high of mood; and her name is Princess Gyda."

"Oh, let us reach that hall soon!" cried Prince Harald. "How soon shall we reach it, Ross?"

"By dawn," said Ross the Finn. "By the sunset door we went out from King Alfdan's hall. By the sunrise door we will go into King Eric's."

On, on, on, as swift and as light as birds, they sped over the ice. The black sky grew less dark. The sharp stars faded.

Soon the sky began to grow pale. The forms of the trees at the edge of the lake began to grow clear.

And at last, in a gap in the line of the trees, they saw the big black bulk of a hall.

"Is that King Eric's hall?" asked Prince Harald.

"It is, my prince," said Ross the Finn. "You see, a ten-year-old prince can skate from Hadland to Ordland!"

The sun rose as they drew near. They saw the sunrise door, the east door of the hall, swing wide. Out of it came a man, tall and big of frame. With him came a small girl. Side by side they stood at the sunrise door, to greet the sun as it rose.

"Is that King Eric?" asked Prince Harald.

"It is," said Ross the Finn.

"Is that Princess Gyda with him?" asked Prince Harald.

"It is," said Ross the Finn.

"She stands with her father to greet the sun as I stand each dawn with mine," said Prince Harald. "Ross, if my father has not yet found that I have left his hall, he will find it out now, when I do not go to greet the sun with him."

They drew in to the edge of the ice. It was midwinter; yet as loud and sweet as if it were spring sang the birds in King Eric's hall thatch to greet the sun.

Ross the Finn bent and took off his skates. Then up the bank of the lake he went to King Eric.

Prince Harald did as the Finn did.

He saw that King Eric was big and bluff and brown of skin and red of hair and beard. He saw how his red hair and his red beard blew about him in the wind.

He saw how Princess Gyda's long red hair blew up to mix with King Eric's red beard.

"King Eric," said Ross the Finn, "I bring you Prince Harald of Hadland."

The eyes of the small prince met the eyes of the big king. Prince Harald saw that King Eric's eyes were merry.

But he saw, too, that they had the look of eyes that saw more than other eyes saw.

"If Gyda will but be true to Gyda," said King Eric, "it

is not Prince Harald of Hadland that you bring me, but King Harald of Norway."

Then he bent, and took Prince Harald's small hand in his own big brown fist.

"I am glad for Norway's sake to see you, Harald Hair-Fair," he said. "So is Gyda, here, and so are the birds in my hall thatch. Gyda, take your guest in and wash his hands and feet. Give him to eat and to drink; then let him sleep. When you have slept, Harald Hair-Fair, you shall help us to eat up your father's yule feast."

Princess Gyda shook back her long red hair. She put out her hand and took the hand of Prince Harald.

She led him in by the sunrise door into King Eric's hall.

# How his uncle went
# after Prince Harald

Just at the time when Princess Gyda led Prince Harald
by the sunrise door into King Eric's hall, at the far end
of the lake King Alfdan the Black went out by his own
sunrise door.

Queen Ragnild and Prince Guthorm went out with
him, to greet the sun. But Prince Harald was not to be
seen.

"Our Hair-Fair sleeps late today," said Prince Guthorm. "I will fetch him."

For it was Prince Guthorm's way to try to shield
the young prince from the black moods of King
Alfdan.

Prince Guthorm was a grown man now, as brave as
he was wise, and as wise as he was brave. Such was
his skill in swordcraft that from the day he was sixteen
years old, he had led King Alfdan's men.

In he went to Prince Harald's sleeping room. Prince
Harald was not in his bed; he was not in his room; he
was not in the hall.

"It may be that he went out to groom his steed," said
Prince Guthorm.

And out he went to seek him in the stable.

By the dim dawn light, as he went, he saw footprints
in the snow. Two sets ran side by side. He saw that
they were the prints of a boy and of a man small and
slight of frame.

He saw that they came from the sunset door of the

hall. So he went to it, and tried it. At his light push, it swung open.

Back he went to track the footprints. From the sunset door they led down to the rim of the lake. At the edge of the ice they came to an end; but at that same spot began skate marks, two sets that ran south side by side.

They were fresh made since last sunset.

He saw that they ran to the Place of the Cattle Branding. But all the way to the foot of Haki's grave mound, the vast sheet of blue-white ice was bare. No small prince and no small slight man were to be seen on the ice.

Prince Guthorm went back and told all this to King Alfdan. King Alfdan's looks grew black.

"Two sets of skate marks?" he cried. "Find out who went with the lad!"

Prince Guthorm set his horn to his lips, and blew the note for the roll call. At the sound, his men ran and fell in, rank on rank. No gap in any rank was to be seen.

"Is the hall just as it was left last night?" asked Prince Guthorm.

His right-hand man told him: "Lord, the table lacks one dish, one ale horn, and one meat dagger."

"Did no man wake in the night?" asked Prince Guthorm. "Did no man hear any stir in the hall?" But no man had.

"Lord," said his right-hand man again, "well-fed men sleep deep."

"But not so men who must fast," said Prince Guthorm. "So it may be that Ross the Finn can tell us more."

He strode up the hall to the door of the cave room.

He cried in a tone that rang along the roof: "Ross, did you hear men in the hall in the night?"

Each man in the hall held his breath. So still was it in the hall that the stir of a foot on straw was as loud as a crack of thunder. But no sound came forth from the dark cave room.

Prince Guthorm slid back the bar of the door of the cave room. He flung the door wide.

"Ross!" he cried again. "Did you hear men in the hall in the night?" But still no sound came from the dark cave room. Prince Guthorm bent to stare into the gloom.

"Saxo, bring me a torch!" he said to his right-hand man.

Saxo ran to light a pine brand and to bring it to Prince Guthorm. By its red glow the prince saw the thongs that had bound Ross the Finn hand and foot. They lay, cut, on the floor. By them lay a dish, an ale horn, and a meat dagger.

Save for them, the cave room was bare.

From lip to lip down the hall flew the news: "Ross the Finn has fled! It is with Ross the Finn that our small Hair-Fair has fled!"

The eyes of King Alfdan were aflash with rage as they met the eyes of Prince Guthorm.

"So it was to steal my son from me," he cried, "that the Finn came to my hall!"

"Yet it may still be," said Prince Guthorm, "that our Hair-Fair went with him of his own free will."

"I care not if he did," cried King Alfdan the Black. "Take men, Guthorm, and track them, and bring them both back to me!"

So Guthorm and a band of the king's men set out by sledge to track the skate marks on the ice. Each sledge was drawn by three strong steeds.

Clip-clop, clip-clop, clip-clop, as swift as birds over

154

the ice they went. On and on the tracks led them, till they came to the foot of Haki's grave mound.

Then Prince Guthorm held back his steeds, and held his hand high, to bid his men halt.

"But the tracks go on, lord," said Saxo, his right-hand man.

"They do," said Prince Guthorm. "But do you not see how soft and weak the ice is in the Place of the Cattle Branding?"

"Yet it held under the skates," said Saxo.

"Ice that holds under skate may not hold under sledge," said Prince Guthorm. "We must skirt this weak ice and pick up the skate tracks again when we are past it."

So round the edge of the weak ice went each sledge, to pick up the skate tracks again on the far side of the Place of the Cattle Branding.

Clip-clop, clip-clop, clip-clop, swift as birds on they went. On and on the tracks led them, on and on to the south end of the lake. On and on the tracks led them till they saw, in a gap in the trees a tall hall with a deep thatch of straw.

"We must be on Ordland ice now," said Prince Guthorm to Saxo. "For by the straw thatch I take that to be the hall of King Eric of Ordland."

They saw that the skate marks came to an end at the rim of the lake below King Eric's hall. From the lake they saw two sets of footprints go up the snow of the bank to the sunrise door of the hall. Like the footprints that had led down to the lake from King Alfdan's sunset door, they were the prints of a boy and of a man small and slight of frame.

"So it was two King Eric the Merry that our Hair-Fair fled!" cried Saxo. "How came he to do a thing so odd and so bold?"

"This thing must go deeper than just a small lad's caper," said Prince Guthorm. "I think we shall find the hand of fate in it."

Forth from his sledge went Prince Guthorm, and up from the edge of the lake to the hall. The birds in the hall thatch sang loud as he blew a blast on the guest horn.

The door of the hall swung wide. Men came out to meet and greet him. Into the hall and up to the high seat was Prince Guthorm led with joy.

On his high seat sat King Eric, big and brown and merry. On two stools at his feet sat the small Princess Gyda and the small Prince Harald. Red head and fair head were bent over chessmen of gold and of silver. King Eric's red bush of a beard swept now fair head and now red head as he bent to help each child in turn.

That red beard shook with mirth as King Eric made jest after jest. Small prince and small princess shook with mirth under it. All the hall was loud with the mirth of King Eric's men.

It did Prince Guthorm good to see the face of the small Prince Harald so bright and gay.

But Prince Harald's bright face fell when Prince Guthorm told King Eric he had been sent to take his nephew back.

"It is not my will to go back yet, Uncle Guthorm. King Eric is a merry host; I like right well to be his guest. And Gyda is the best playmate I have ever had."

King Eric gave a merry shrug.

"If he will not go with you of his own free will, Prince Guthorm," he said, "I must not let him go at all. For he is my guest, and the guest law must be kept."

"And Ross the Finn, King Eric?"

"He, too, is my guest, and the guest law must be

kept," said King Eric. "But stay this day and this night with us, and help us eat and drink King Alfdan's yule feast. At dawn you shall go back and beg King Alfdan for me to let his son stay here in Ordland till the spring."

Glad was Prince Guthorm to stay that day and that night in a hall so full of gay cheer. Long was it since he had spent a day so merry. Jest for jest he gave back to cap the jests of King Eric. Each time, the hall rang with the men's mirth. Each time, Prince Harald's face lit up. Each time, Princess Gyda shook back her long red hair to smile at him.

"Harald Hair-Fair," she said, "right well do I like your uncle, as you right well like my father. I will share my father with you, if you will share your uncle with me."

"Let us handfast that!" cried the small prince, and took her hand in his. "Now your father shall be my father, and my uncle shall be your uncle, as long as we all live."

"What if it is not my will?" asked Prince Guthorm, with a twinkle.

"Oh, but it is your will, Uncle Guthorm!" cried Princess Gyda.

"The birds in my hall thatch sing that it is fate's will," said King Eric. "Yet it still lies with a man's own will if he will do fate's will or no."

"Will our Hair-Fair, think you?"

"With Gyda to sting him on, I think he will," said King Eric. "If so, this small lad who pulls this small girl's hair will be the first king of all Norway."

"How will so vast a thing come to pass?" Prince Guthorm asked.

"So high a fate can be born only of much pain," said

King Eric. "All save three small parts of Norway must be won with bloodshed."

"And those three parts?" asked Prince Guthorm.

"Hadland, Ring-Rik, and Ordland," King Eric told him. "Hadland is his by birth. Ring-Rik is his by gift — by your own gift. Ordland will be his by gift — by my own gift. But that will not be till all the rest is won."

"My gift to start, your gift to end," said Prince Guthorm.

"And all the rest the pang and clang of battle, sing my birds," King Eric said.

# How Haki's death-wish came true

Next day, Prince Guthorm was up at dawn. With King Eric, Prince Harald, and Princess Gyda, out by the sunrise door he went to greet the sun.

Then down the snowbank to the edge of the lake they went to the sledge train. Prince Harald ran to help Saxo hold back the steeds of the first sledge as Prince Guthorm got into it. Princess Gyda ran to tuck his furs about him.

"Take care that the ice holds, Uncle Guthorm," said Prince Harald.

"Yes, Uncle Guthorm, take care that the ice holds," said Princess Gyda.

"When Ross and I came past Haki's grave mound," said the prince, "Ross saw with troll-sight that the Place of the Cattle Branding will soon be a grave."

"And not only Ross," said King Eric. "For the birds in my hall thatch sing that a breath of death steals forth from Haki's grave mound. Take care."

"Care will I take," said Prince Guthorm with a smile.

Then off over the ice went his sledge. Clip-clop, clip-clop, clip-clop, rang the hoofs of his steeds on the ice. And back to Hadland with him went his sledge train of king's men.

When Haki's grave mound came in sight, they took care to skirt the soft, weak ice in the Place of the Cattle Branding. So all came back safe and sound to the hall with the golden roof.

When Prince Guthorm came up from the lake and into the hall, King Alfdan had just begun to twist his bow a new bowstring. He saw Prince Guthorm come in, no Finn and no small prince with him. His eyebrows drew into a black frown, and so hard did he jerk the bowstring that its snap sang down the hall like a harp string.

Prince Guthorm told him how he had found the small prince with King Eric, safe and well and gay.

"And King Eric begs you will let our Hair-Fair stay with him till spring," he said.

With a face as black as a thundercloud, King Alfdan threw down his bow and strode down his hall.

"Get out my sledge!" he cried to his men. "If my son will not come when I send for him, I will go and fetch him myself."

"I beg you to let him stay, Alfdan," said Prince Guthorm. "It is good for a lad of his age to see new lands and new ways."

"You are too soft with him, Guthorm," said King Alfdan. "Fetch him back I will."

"Lord," said Torlef the Wise, "I too beg you not to go."

King Alfdan swung around on his wise man.

"You, too, Torlef?" he cried. "Are you then hand in hand with Guthorm to cross my will?"

"Lord," said Torlef, "Prince Guthorm begs you for Prince Harald's sake. I beg you for your own. Think, lord — how old are you?"

"I am forty winters old, as you well know," said King Alfdan. "But why ask of that now?"

"Forty winters old," said Torlef, "was Haki the Wolf's Head when he died on the ice. Do you not call to mind the death-wish he cried on you then?"

"If you do not, Alfdan, I do," said Prince Guthorm. "This is what Haki cried in his death hour: 'You have won the Princess Ragnild, Alfdan the Black. But when you reach the age that I am now, take heed, lest the ice bring you to your death as now it brings me to mine'."

"Of Haki in the flesh I had no fear," cried the king. "Of Haki dead I have less. Go to Ordland this day I will."

"Alfdan!" cried Queen Ragnild. "Tempt not a dead man's death-wish. Let Harald stay with King Eric till spring. Then we can all go by boat to fetch him back. Do not risk the ice when the wind is so mild it may well bring a thaw."

"No thaw has set in yet," said King Alfdan. "Go to Ordland this day I will."

And out he went, and down the snowbank to his sledge.

Prince Guthorm went with him down to the edge of the lake.

"It is true that no thaw has set in yet, Alfdan," he said. "But keep clear of the Place of the Cattle Branding. At the foot of Haki's grave mound, the ice is weak and soft; and Ross the Finn saw with troll-sight that it is soon to be a grave."

"Tell me not of the Finn!" cried King Alfdan. "Was it not he who set my son to cross my will?" And in so red a rage did he set off that he gave no heed to what Prince Guthorm had said, but drove his steeds hard due south in a beeline for Ordland.

His whiplash sent his steeds on far ahead of the rest of the sledge train. His sledge sped on alone. And alone he came to the Place of the Cattle Branding.

So full of rage was he still that he gave no heed to the ice. He did not see, as Prince Guthorm had seen, how the cattle dung had sunk in and made the ice soft and weak. He did not see how the marks of Prince Guthorm's sledge train went round on the sound ice. He saw only that the track of the skates still went on.

And on he still went after them.

With the loud clip-clop of his steeds in his ears he did not hear the ice crack. Too late to pull up his steeds in time, he saw a black pit yawn in the blue-white ice. He felt the sledge heel over. Down he was shot into a deep black pit of ice-cold water.

The steeds began to thrash and to rear in the water, to seek for a firm foothold. Under the ice they went. Under the ice with them they drew King Alfdan the Black.

His sledge train drew up at the edge of the Place of the Cattle Branding. Each man left his sledge and crept on hands and knees to the rim of the black pit.

"I will go in after him," said Saxo. "Tie a lifeline to my belt, and pull in hard when I tug it."

To Saxo's belt they tied a lifeline, and held it tight. Into the water he went, and they saw the deep black water close over his head.

They felt him tug. They drew the lifeline in. When he came up, he had King Alfdan limp in his arms. They took the dead king from him. They drew Saxo onto the ice.

Back to the sledge train at the foot of Haki's grave mound they bore the dead king. Back they bore Saxo, limp but still alive. Back sped the sledge train to the hall with the golden roof.

Sad and slow rang the steps of the men as they bore the dead king up the long hall, and laid him at the feet of Queen Ragnild.

Queen Ragnild knelt and wept over him as with white hands she made smooth his wet black hair. But Torlef the Wise stood with grave face and bit his lip, his hand on his beard, for he saw the rocks and the reefs that lay ahead.

He said to Prince Guthorm: "Come back now Prince Harald must. But your place is with the queen; she will need you in her loss. So this time it is I who must go and bring our small king home."

So over the ice sped the sledge train again to Ordland. As it drew in at the rim of the lake, Torlef the Wise saw King Eric come to the door of his hall. As still as a stout brown tree he stood in the snow, to catch the drift of the song the birds sang so loud in his hall thatch.

Up the snowbank to him came Torlef. He told him all that had come to pass.

"Your Hair-Fair and my Gyda went up to the hills, to ski with Ross the Finn," King Eric said. "I will send men to bring him to you. And now, come in and eat."

As they sat at meat, Torlef said: "See how the ill wish Haki cried in his death hour the king's own rage has made come true! And see now the ill fate it brings for Hadland and for Ring-Rik! For a strong king has died in his prime and has left his two lands to a lad but ten years old!"

"Yet with you and Queen Ragnild and Prince Guthorm to teach him how to rule," said King Eric, "even so small a lad can be a strong king too."

"It is the king's men, lord, who will not wish to take so small a lad for king," said Torlef. "If Prince Guthorm will take it, the crown of both lands is his."

King Eric sat with his big red beard in his big brown hands.

"Perhaps that may be his men's will, but not his," said King Eric.

"For it is his own dream to help the dream in the pigsty to come true. And Harald Hair-Fair must needs

164

first be king of his own two small lands if he is to end as king of all Norway."

"Think you he will so end?" asked Torlef.

"It was a fate he might well have let slip his mind," said King Eric, "had he not met my Gyda. But my child has red hair, Torlef; she will sting him to reach out to what fate wills for him if he will but will it, too. To that end I made my plans for them to meet this yuletide. That, Torlef, is why you now eat of King Alfdan's yuletide feast."

Then Torlef saw Ross the Finn come into the hall.

And with him, hand in hand, eyes bright and cheeks aglow, came the small Prince Harald and the small Princess Gyda.

Then Torlef told Prince Harald of his father's death. Prince Harald laid his small hand in the big fist of King Eric.

"I must go back to my mother; she will need me," he said.

Then he threw out his arms and gave Gyda a big hug.

"Never will I forget you, Gyda," he said. "See that you do not forget me. For as soon as I am of age to wed, I shall send for you to come and be my bride."

Gyda gave a toss of her red head.

"The man I wed," said she, "must be king of more than two small lands!"

"What then must he be king of?" asked Prince Harald.

"All Norway," said the princess.

"Then that will I be!" said the prince.

Then back he went with Torlef to the hall with the golden roof.

# How the dream
# in the pigsty came true

Glad was Queen Ragnild when her son came home.
Glad, too, was his uncle, Prince Guthorm. But the king's
men stood back, and gave the lad cold looks.

"Be honest with me, Prince Guthorm," said Torlef
the Wise. "If your men so will, is it your will to take
the crown?"

"My will it is not," said Prince Guthorm. "And if it is
my men's will, such it shall not be for long."

That night, as his men lay down to sleep, he said
to them: "The day will soon be set when we shall
take Prince Harald as our king. Let each of you rub
his helmet and shield and coat of mail bright, to
match the new gold arm rings he will give you on that
day."

He saw how each man's face grew dark at this. Each
man began to growl in his beard.

"A lad ten winters old is no king for us, lord," said
Saxo.

Said the next man: "We need a grown man for king,
wise in the ways of war, lord, and with skill in swordcraft."

Then all the men gave a shout: "We need you, lord!
It is our will, Prince Guthorm, to take you for our
king!" Prince Guthorm's eyes went from face to face.
His own face was stern. He stood still, and did not
speak.

"Lord, the land of Ring-Rik is your land by right,"

cried Saxo. "When your father, King Sigurd the Hart, was slain, you were as small a lad as Prince Harald is now. So you did not take it then. Now the time is ripe for you to do so."

"Men!" cried Prince Guthorm then. "All of you sat in this hall when Ragnild my sister wedded King Alfdan. Do you call to mind what I said then? If you cannot tell me, I will tell you."

Then Saxo said: "Lord, you said this: 'I bring a vow as a bride gift. The land of Ring-Rik is mine, but I vow never to be its king. I give it to you, Alfdan and Ragnild, to add to your own land of Hadland. For it seems to me that when two small lands have each a king, both lands are weak. But when two small lands have the same king, both lands are strong'."

"That vow I have kept," said Prince Guthorm. "That vow I will still keep. Take our Hair-Fair as king of both lands, and you will find he has a high fate in store. As for the lad's age, that is a thing time will soon cure."

"And till then, lord?" asked Saxo.

And Prince Guthorm told the men: "Till then, Queen Ragnild and Lord Torlef will rule for him in things of state and teach him statecraft. I will lead his men as I led his father's; and we, his men, will teach him swordcraft and the ways of war. Men, I think that out of this small lad we shall make a strong king!" At that, a cheer went up from the men.

"On such terms, lord," they cried, "we will take our Hair-Fair as king!" So, on the day set by Torlef, the small Prince Harald sat in his father's big high seat. And one by one his men came up the long hall to him, and put a big hand in his small ones, and took him to be king.

The hall was bright with cloth-of-gold that day. Bright was each helmet, each shield, each coat of mail. Bright were the gold arm rings the new king gave his men that day.

Rich was the feast that night, as the men sat at the long table, ate and drank and made merry.

Now the slow years went by, and King Harald Hair-Fair grew up.

All went well all this time with his two small lands of Hadland and Ring-Rik. Yet it was no thanks to him that this was so, for he left it to others to rule them. Nor did he show any wish to add other lands to his own.

As time went on in this way, his men said to each other: "Is this the strong king, wise in the ways of war, we were to have had? This is no king, but a milksop who moons in the hall from dawn to dusk."

And Queen Ragnild said to herself with a sigh: "When will this small thorn, that my son is still, grow into the vast tree of my dream?"

And even Torlef the Wise shook his head, and said to Prince Guthorm: "Was not Harald Hair-Fair born to do more than this, to be more than this? The years go by, yet he lifts no hand to make the dream in the pigsty come true!"

"Put your trust in King Eric, Torlef," said Prince Guthorm. "Did he not say Princess Gyda had stung our Hair-Fair to stretch out his hand to his fate? We shall yet see that in due time this he will do."

So the time came when King Harald was of age to wed.

He sent for his uncle, Prince Guthorm. He sent for his wise man, Torlef. He told them: "When I was ten winters old, I chose Princess Gyda of Ordland to be my bride. Go now to her father, King Eric, and ask her hand of him for me."

Prince Guthorm and Torlef the Wise took a band of the king's men. They took a ship with red ropes and with sails of blue and white silk. And in this they went south down the lake to the hall of King Eric of Ordland.

King Eric was still big and stout and brown and merry. His red head and his red beard had still not one white hair.

When they told him why they came, his red beard began to wag with mirth.

"He sent you to ask her hand of me?" he cried. "Never tell Gyda that! Her hair is red, as you well know, and she is apt to flare up as a pine brand! She is a maid with a mind of her own, a maid with a will of her own. Let us find that mind out now."

He led them up the stone stairs that went from the hall to her bower.

In her bower, Princess Gyda sat at a silver loom, and wove bright cloth-of-gold. Her hair, as she bent to the loom, was like a wave of flame.

Her silver shuttle flew to and fro. From edge to edge of the cloth it drew the gold thread with a flash like that of a spear.

She rose as they came in, and they saw that she was as tall and as swift and as strong as a spear herself.

"Uncle Guthorm!" she cried.

And she came to him and took both his hands in hers.

"Is it to see my father or is it to see me that you come after so many years?" she asked.

Just in time, Prince Guthorm saw the twinkle in King Eric's eye.

"To see you, Gyda," he said. "Do you call to mind how, when you were ten years old, Harald Hair-Fair told you of his wish to wed you? Now you are both of age to wed, and he sends me to ask you if you will now be his bride."

She threw up her bright head and shook her red hair back in just her old way as a child.

"You were not with us, Uncle Guthorm," she said, "but Lord Torlef was. So he knows, if you do not, that I told Harald Hair-Fair then not to send for me till he had put all Norway under him. Now both of you go back, and tell him that again."

"But stay and eat first," said the merry King Eric.

As the three sat at meat, he said: "My red Gyda has the fire that Harald Hair-Fair lacks. Sure fire he needs if he is to reach out to grasp his fate. Tell him from me that when he has won the rest of Norway, Ordland shall be his as my bride-gift."

So, in the ship with red ropes and with blue and white silk sails, Prince Guthorm and Torlef the Wise went north up the lake to the hall with the golden roof.

"Think you he will flare into red rage when we tell him?" Torlef asked Prince Guthorm. "Or fall into a black mood, like his father?"

"I do not know," said Prince Guthorm. "He is my own sister's son; yet I feel that much must lie deep in him that I have not yet seen."

So they came to King Harald and told him: "Princess Gyda bids us tell you she will not wed you till you have put all Norway under you."

King Harald did not flare into red rage. Nor did he fall into a black mood, like his father. He sat still for a time on his high seat, his flax-pale head on his hand.

Then he said: "I owe Gyda thanks. For she brings to my mind things I need to think of. Here and now I make this vow: That I will not clip nor cut my hair till I have put all the land of Norway under me."

Then was Torlef glad that Gyda had stung Harald to reach out to grasp his high fate. And glad was Queen Ragnild to see the small thorn of her dream start to grow at last. And Prince Guthorm cried, for his own self and for all the king's men: "Harald, it is with joy we hear you vow a vow so kingly!"

From that day King Harald Hair-Fair let his fair hair grow. He did not clip it; he did not cut it.

So fast it grew, so long it grew, that the time came when his flax-pale locks were as long as Gyda's red ones. So fast it grew, so long it grew, that the time came when his flax-pale locks were as long as the long fair lock in King Alfdan's dream.

And now just to see this man with the long pale hair at the head of his men struck fear into his foes. For as his hair grew in length, so did he grow in strength, and in skill, and in wisdom. He grew wise in the ways of men and of wars; he grew in skill in swordcraft and statecraft; he grew into a strong king.

With Prince Guthorm he led out the men of Hadland and Ring-Rik to win land after land. In battle after battle the swords sang and the spears thundered. In battle after battle coats of mail were cleft and shields were bent and helmets rent, and blades grew hot, and fields grew red.

As in Queen Ragnild's dream, the roots of the tree that was King Harald were roots as red as blood.

And many, many were the roots that had to be torn up that King Harald's might be firm and strong. Many kings and many king's men fell in battle. Many came to King Harald, to be his men. Many who held still to the old ways had to flee from Norway, to hew out a new life in new lands.

Others fled to sea, and, as Vikings, set sail in long ships to rob and to raid other lands.

After three years, King Harald Hair-Fair was the only free king save one left in all Norway. The other free king was King Eric the Merry of Ordland.

Then back to his hall with its golden roof came King Harald Hair-Fair. He cut his long locks short. He sent for Prince Guthorm and Torlef the Wise.

To them he said: "Now go again to Princess Gyda. Tell her that now I have all Norway under me."

So again Prince Guthorm and Torlef took a band of the king's men. Again they took a ship with red ropes and sails of blue and white silk. And in it again they went south down the lake to the hall of King Eric of Ordland.

Gladly, then, did Princess Gyda go back with them, her hair like locks of flame. Gladly, too, went King Eric, big and stout and brown and merry, his red beard blown this way and that as he stood in the prow of the ship.

Gladly did King Harald and Queen Ragnild meet them. Glad and rich and merry was the bride feast. And gladly did King Eric keep his vow, and give to King Harald his own small land of Ordland as a bride-gift.

And now began the long, long years of joy and plenty, the years that in Queen Ragnild's dream were the trunk of the tree as green as grass. Now all the land of Norway was at rest. The crops grew ripe. The barns were full.

When at last King Harald Hair-Fair died, he was

eighty-three years old. His flax-pale locks had for many years been as white as snow, as white as the twigs on the tree in Queen Ragnild's dream.

In this wise did Harald Hair-Fair come to be the first king to hold sway over all Norway.

And in this wise did Queen Ragnild's dream and the dream in the pigsty come true.

*Other books by Isabel Wyatt*

# King Beetle-Tamer
## and other light-hearted wonder tales

This collection of fifteen fairy tales is written by a `weaver of magic.' The tales are filled with unicorns and fairies, magic and wonder. And in this magic world the princess often rescues the prince! *(Age 8-11)*

# The Seven-Year-Old Wonder Book

These magical tales take us through the highlights of Sylvia's year, through festivals and her seventh birthday. *(Age 7+)*

# The Book of Fairy Princes

A collection of beautifully-told stories which transport us to ivory towers, great forests, golden lands, and kingdoms of beautiful colours. *(Age 8-11)*